S0-BYT-870

High
Wizardry

Discard
NHCPL

NEW HANOVER COUNTY
PUBLIC LIBRARY
201 CHESTNUT STREET
WILMINGTON, N. C. 28401

Also by Diane Duane

SO YOU WANT TO BE A WIZARD

DEEP WIZARDRY

High
Wizardry

★ ★ ★

Diane Duane

**Delacorte
Press**

Published by
Delacorte Press
Bantam Doubleday Dell Publishing Group, Inc.
666 Fifth Avenue
New York, New York 10103

Excerpt from "Birches" by Robert Frost: Copyright 1916 by Holt, Rinehart and Winston and renewed 1944 by Robert Frost. Reprinted from THE POETRY OF ROBERT FROST edited by Edward Connery Lathem, by permission of Henry Holt and Company, Inc.

Excerpts from "Running Alone" by Steve Perry, John Bettis, Duane Hitchings, and Craig Krampf: © 1984 Street Talk Tunes, WB Music Corp. (ASCAP), Hitchings Music, Phosphene Music (BMI). All Rights Reserved. Used by permission.

Copyright © 1990 by Diane Duane

All rights reserved. No part of this book may be reproduced or transmitted in any form or by any means, electronic or mechanical, including photocopying, recording or by any information storage and retrieval system, without the written permission of the Publisher, except where permitted by law.

The trademark Delacorte Press® is registered in the U.S. Patent and Trademark Office.

Library of Congress Cataloging in Publication Data

Duane, Diane.
    High wizardry / by Diane Duane.
       p.   cm.
    Summary: When her younger sister uses the family computer with its special wizard software to travel to worlds light years away, Nita uses her wizardry to try and find her.
    ISBN 0-385-29983-4
    [1. Fantasy. 2. Science fiction. 3. Computers—Fiction.]
I. Title.
PZ7.D84915Hi   1990
[Fic]—dc20   89-34818   CIP   AC

Manufactured in the United States of America

April 1990

10 9 8 7 6 5 4 3 2 1

BG

For my dear master,
from someone nearly as surprised

ACKNOWLEDGMENTS AND WARNINGS

Ben Yalow, chief of Academic Computing at CUNY and old friend, contributed much valuable advice on the subtleties of both AI and hardware, all of which contributed to this book one way or another.

Dan Oehlsen knows what he contributed to the effort: a great courtesy, for which many thanks.

Cheerful thanks and good wishes go to the members of the IBM PC Professional and IBM PC Novice Special Interest Groups on CompuServe, who were instrumental in assisting the writer in hitting her deadline. Friends, may your files never be busy!

And thanks, too, to the many members of the CompuServe Science Fiction and Fantasy SIG, whose nightly inquiries about their former Assistant SysOp's new book kept her going.

The author wishes to warn her readers that attempts to reproduce effects described in this book using their own computers may result in extreme frustration, or in damage to their software or hardware, or in violation of their end-user agreements, or all of the above at once: and for said results the author declines to be held legally responsible.

I'd like to get away from Earth awhile
And then come back to it and begin over.
May no fate willfully misunderstand me
And half grant what I wish and snatch me away
Not to return. Earth's the right place for love:
I don't know where it's likely to go better.

Robert Frost, "Birches"

Where, except in the present, can the Eternal be met?

C. S. Lewis, "Historicism"

Those who refuse to serve the Powers,
become the tools of the Powers.
Those who agree to serve the Powers,
Themselves *become* the Powers.

Beware the Choice! Beware refusing it!

Book of Night with Moon,
Tetrastych xiv: "Fire over Heaven"

High
Wizardry

Initialization

"Hey, there's somebody in the driveway! It's a truck! Mom! Mom, the computer's here!"

The first sound Nita heard that morning was her little sister's shrieking. Nita winced and scrunched herself up into a ball under the covers. Then she muttered six syllables, a very simple spell, and soundproofed her room against her sister's noise.

Blessed silence fell. Unfortunately the spell also killed the buzzing of the locusts and the singing of the birds outside the open window. And Nita liked birds. She opened her eyes, blinking at the bright summer sun coming in the window, and sighed.

Nita said one more syllable. The mute-spell came undone, letting in the noise of doors opening and shutting, and Dairine shrieking instructions and suggestions at the immediate planet. Outside the window a catbird was sitting in the elm tree, screaming, "Thief! Thief!" in an enthusiastic but substandard imitation of a blue jay.

So much for sleeping late, Nita thought. She got up and went over to the dresser by the window, pulled a drawer open and rummaged in it for a T-shirt and shorts. "Morning, Birdbrain," she said as she pulled out a "Live Aid" T-shirt.

The catbird hopped down to a branch of the elm right outside Nita's window. "Bob-white! Bob-white!" it sang at the top of its lungs.

"What's a quail doing in a tree?" Nita said. She pulled the T-shirt on. "Listen to those locusts! Hot one today, huh?"

"Highs in the nineties," the bird sang. "Cheer up! Cheer up!"

"Robins are for spring," Nita said. "I'm more in the mood for penguins at the moment. . . ."

"What's up?"

"Enough with the imitations! I need you to take a message for me. Wizards' business. I'll leave you something nice. Half of one of Mom's muffins? Huh?"

The catbird poured out several delighted bars of song that started as a phoebe's call and ended as the five-note theme from *E.T.*

"Good," Nita said. "Then here's something new to sing." She had been speaking all along in the Speech of wizards, the language everything alive

★ 2 ★

understands. Now she added music to it, singing random notes with the words. "Kit, you wanna see a disaster? Come on over here and watch my folks try to hook up the Apple."

The bird cocked an interested eye at her. "You need it again?" Nita said.

"'Kit, you wanna see a disaster?'"

"That's my boy. You remember the way?"

In a whir of white-barred wings, the catbird was gone.

"Must be hungry," Nita said to herself, pulling on her shorts, and then socks and sneakers. While pulling a sneaker on, she glanced at the top of the dresser. There among the stickers and the brushes and combs, under the new Alan Parsons album, lay her wizard's manual.

That by itself wasn't so strange; she'd left it there yesterday afternoon. But it was open; she didn't remember having left it that way. Nita leaned over, tying the sneaker, and looked at the page. The Wizards' Oath—Nita smiled. It didn't seem like only a few months ago that she'd first read and taken that Oath herself: it felt more like years. February, was it? she thought. No, March. Joanne and her crew chased me into the library. And beat the crap out of me later. But I didn't care. I'd found this—

Nita sighed and flipped the book back to the Oath. Trouble came with wizardry. But other things came too—

Whamwhamwham!

★ 3 ★

Nita didn't even need to turn around to see who was pounding on her door as it banged open. "Come in!" Nita said, and glared at Dairine, who already *was* in.

"It's here!"

"I would never have known," Nita said, dropping the Parsons album back on top of the manual. "Dari, sometimes people like to sleep on a Saturday, y'know?"

"When there's a *computer* here? Nita, sometimes you're such a *spud.*"

Nita folded her arms and leaned against the dresser, ready to start a lecture. Her sister, unfortunately, took all the fun out of it by mocking Nita's position and folded arms, leaning against the doorjamb. Funny how someone so little could look so threatening: a little red-haired eleven-year-old stick of a thing in an Admiral Ackbar T-shirt, with a delicate face and watery gray eyes. Problem was, there was someone smart behind those eyes. Someone *too* smart.

Nita let out an annoyed breath. "I won't kill you this time," she said.

"I wasn't worried about that," Dairine said. "And you won't turn me into a toad or anything, either, so don't bother trying that line on me. . . . C'mon, let's watch Mom 'n' Dad mess it up." And she was out the door.

Nita made a face. It didn't help that Dairine knew she was a wizard. She would sooner have

★ 4 ★

told her parents about her wizardry than have told Dairine.

Of course, her folks had found out too . . .

Nita headed out the bedroom door and down the stairs.

The living room was full of boxes and packing material, loose-leaf books, and diskette boxes. Only the desk by the window was clean; and on it sat a cream-colored object about the size and shape of a phone book—the keyboard/motherboard console of a shiny new Apple IIIc+. "Harry," Nita's mother was saying, "don't plug anything in, you'll blow it up. Dairine, get out of that. Morning, Nita, there's some pancakes on the stove."

"Okay," Nita said, and headed into the kitchen. While she was still spreading maple syrup between two pancakes, someone banged on the screen door.

"C'mon in," Nita said, her mouth full. "Have a pancake."

Kit came in: Christopher Rodriguez, her fellow-wizard, quick and dark and sharp-eyed, and at thirteen, a year younger than Nita. And also suddenly two inches taller, for he had hit a growth spurt over the summer. Nita couldn't get used to it; she was used to looking down at him. She handed him a pancake.

"A little bird told me there's about to be trouble," Kit said.

"C'mon," Dairine's strident voice came from the living room, "I wanna play Lunar Lander!"

★ 5 ★

" 'About to be?' " Nita said.

Kit grinned around the mouthful of pancake and gestured with his head at the living room, raising his eyebrows.

Nita nodded agreement, her mouth full too, and they headed that way.

"Dairine," Nita's mother was saying, "leave your dad alone." Her mother was sitting cross-legged in jeans and sweatshirt, in the middle of a welter of Styrofoam peanuts and paperwork, going through a loose-leaf binder. "And don't get those manuals out of order, either. Morning, Kit! How're your mom and dad?"

"Fine, Mrs. Callahan. Hi, Mr. Callahan."

"Hi, Kit," said Nita's dad, rather muffled because he was under the desk by the living room window. "Betty, I've got the three-prong plugs in."

"Oh, good. Then you can set up the external monitor . . ."

"When can I play?" Dairine hollered.

"At this rate," said her father, "sometime in the next century. Nita, do something with her, will you?"

"It's a little late for birth control," Kit said in Nita's ear. Nita spluttered with laughter.

Dairine flew at her. "Was that something dirty? I'll get you for that, you—"

Queep! something said. All heads turned; but it was just the computer, which Nita's dad had plugged in. "Harry, you *will* blow it up," Nita's mother said calmly, from down among the cartons. "We haven't finished reading the instructions yet."

"We don't have to, Betty. We didn't connect the hard disk yet, so we—"

Dairine lost interest in killing Nita. "Can I play now?!"

"See, it says in this manual—"

"Yes, but this one is before that one, Harry—"

"But, look, Betty, it says right here—"

Dairine quietly slipped the plastic wrapping off the monitor and slipped it into its notch at the back of the computer, then started connecting the cables to the screen. Nita glanced at Kit, then back toward the kitchen. He grinned agreement.

"Your folks are gonna lock her in a closet or something," Kit said as they got out of the combat zone.

"I hope so . . . that's probably the only way I'm gonna get at it. But it's okay; she won't blow it up. Her science class has a IIIc: that's one of the reasons Mom and Dad got this one. Dari already knows more about it than the teacher does."

Kit rolled his eyes. "Uh-huh," Nita said. "But I'm not gonna let her monopolize *this* toy, lemme tell you. It's a neat little thing—it has the new foldout screen, and batteries—you could put it in a bookbag. I'll show you later. . . . Where's Ponch?"

"Outside. C'mon."

They went out and sat on the side steps. The locusts were buzzing louder than ever as Ponch, Kit's big black mutt, part Border collie, part German shepherd, came bounding up the driveway to them through the green-gold early sunlight. "Oh, Lord, look at his nose," Nita said. "Ponch, you got stung again, you loon."

"I buried a bone," Ponch said in a string of whines and barks as he came up to them. "The bad things bit me."

"His favorite bone-burying place," Kit said, sounding resigned, "has three yellowjacket nests spaced around it. He gets stung faster than I can heal him."

"Brave," Ponch said, resting his chin, with the swollen black nose, on Nita's shoulder, and looking sideways at her for sympathy.

"Dumb," Nita said, scratching him behind the ears. "But brave. Go get a stick, brave guy. I'll throw it." Ponch slurped Nita's face and raced off.

Kit smiled to see him run.

"So what're we doing today? Anything?"

"Well, there's a new show at the planetarium in the city. Something about other galaxies. My folks said I could go if I wanted to."

"Hey, neat. You got enough money?"

"Just."

"Great. I think I've got enough—let me check."

Nita went back into the house, noticing as she passed through the living room that Dairine was already slipping a diskette into the Apple's built-in disk drive, while her oblivious mother and father were still sitting on the floor pointing at different pages in three different manuals, and arguing cheerfully. *Queep!* the computer said from the living room, as Nita got into her room and upended the money jar on the dresser.

There was no pause in the arguing. Sometimes I think they like it, Nita thought, counting the bills. She had enough for the planetarium, and maybe a couple of hot dogs afterward. Nita stuffed the money in her pocket and pushed the jar to the back of the dresser.

—And her eye fell on the record album again. She tipped it up by one corner to look at her wizard's manual, still open to the Oath. She pulled the book out, idly touching the open pages as she held it. *In Life's name, and for Life's sake,* began the small block of type on the right-hand page, *I say that I will use this art only in service of that Life . . .*

Dairine was in here yesterday, Nita thought, skimming down over the words of the Oath. . . . And she was reading this. For a moment Nita was furious at the idea of her sister rummaging around in her things; but the anger didn't last. Maybe, she thought, this isn't so bad after all. She's been pestering me with questions about wizardry ever since she found out there really is such a thing. She thinks it's all excitement. But the Oath is heavy stuff. Maybe it threw a little scare into her with all the stuff about "time's end" and doing what you have to, no matter what. Be a good thing if it did make her back off a little. She's too young for this. . . .

Nita shut the manual, tucked it under her arm and headed out into the living room. Dairine was standing in front of the computer, keying in instructions; the Apple logo came up on the monitor, followed by a screenful of green words too small for Nita to read from across the room. Her mother and father were still deep in the manual. "Mom," Nita said, "Kit and I want to go into the city, to the planetarium, is it okay? Kit's folks said he could."

Nita's mother glanced at her, considering. "Well . . . be back before dark."

"Stay out of Times Square," her father said without looking up, while paging through a manual open in his lap.

"Do you have enough money for the train?" her mother said.

"Mom," Nita said, hefting her wizard's manual in one hand, "I don't think we're going to take the train."

"Oh." Her mother looked dubiously at the book. She had seen more than enough evidence of her daughter's power in the past couple of months: but Nita knew better than to think that her mother was getting comfortable about wizardry, or even used to it. "You're not going into the city to, uh, do something, are you?"

"We're not on assignment, Mom, no. Not for a while, I think, after last time."

"Oh. Well . . . just you be careful, Neets. Wizards are a dime a dozen as far as I'm concerned, but daughters . . ."

Nita's father looked up at that. "Stay out of trouble," he said, and meant it.

"Yes, sir."

"Now, Betty, look right here. It says very plainly, 'Do *not* use disk without first—' "

"That's *software*, Harry. They mean the *diskette*, not the disk *drive*—"

Nita hurried out through the kitchen before her folks could change their minds. Kit was evidently thinking along the same lines, since he was standing in the middle of the sandy place by the backyard gate, using the stick Ponch had brought him to draw a wizard's transit circle on the ground. "I sent Ponch home," he said, setting various symbols around the circumference of the circle.

"Okay." Nita stepped in beside him. "Where you headed? The Grand Central worldgate?"

"No, there are delays there this morning. The book says to use Penn Station instead. What time have you got?"

Nita squinted up at the Sun. "Nine thirty-five."

"Show-off. Use the watch; I need the Naval Observatory time."

"Nine thirty-three and twenty seconds," Nita said, scowling at her Timex, *"now."*

"Not bad. Let's haul it before—"

"What are you doing!" yelled Nita's father, inside the house. Nita and Kit both jumped guiltily, then looked at each other. Nita sighed.

"Too late," Kit said.

At nine thirty-three and twenty-eight seconds, the screen door opened and Dairine was propelled firmly out of it. Nita's father put his head out after Dairine, and looked up the driveway. "Take her with you," he said to Nita, and meant that too.

"Yes, sir," Nita said, trying not to sound surly as the screen door slammed shut. Kit rolled his eyes and slowly began adding another set of symbols to those already inside the circle. Dairine scuffed over to them, looking at least as annoyed as Nita felt.

"Well," Dairine said, "I guess I'm stuck with you."

"Get in," Kit said, sounding resigned. "Don't step on the lines."

"And try not to freak out too much, okay?" Nita said.

Dairine stepped over the bounds of the circle and stood there with her arms folded, glaring at Nita.

"What a great time we're all going to have," Kit said, opening his manual. He began to read in the wizardly Speech, fast. Nita looked away from her sister and let Kit handle it.

The air around them began to sing—the same note ears sing when they've been in a noisy place too long; but this singing got louder, not softer, as seconds passed. Nita had the mild satisfaction of

★ 12 ★

seeing Dairine start to look nervous at that, and at the slow breeze beginning around them when everywhere else the summer air was still. The breeze got stronger, dust around them whipped and scattered in it, the sound scaled up until it blotted out almost everything else. And despite her annoyance, Nita suddenly got lost in the old familiar exhilaration of magic working. From memory—for she and Kit had worked this spell together many times— she lifted her voice in the last chorus of it, where the words came in a rush, and the game and skill of the spell lay in matching your partner's cadence exactly. Kit dropped not a syllable as Nita came in, but flashed her a wry grin, matching her word for word for the last ten seconds; they ended together on one word that was half laugh, half shout of triumph. And on the word, the air around them cracked like thunder and struck inward from all directions, like a blow—

The wind stilled and the dust settled, and they found themselves in the last aisle of a small chain bookstore, next to a door with a hand-lettered sign that said EMPLOYEES ONLY. Kit put his manual away, and he and Nita were brushing themselves off when that door popped open and a small sandy-haired man with inquiring eyes looked out at them. "Something fall down out here? No? . . . You need some help?"

"Uh," Nita and Kit said, still in unison.

★ 13 ★

"X-Men comics," said Dairine, not missing a beat.

"Up front on the right, in the rack," said the small man, and vanished through his door again.

"Hope they have the new annual," Dairine said, brushing dust off her shorts and Admiral Ackbar shirt, and heading for the front of the store.

Kit and Nita glanced ruefully at each other and went after her. It looked like it was going to be a long day.

Passwords

Like so many other human beings, Dairine had made her first major decision about life and the world quite early; at the age of three, in fact. She had seen Nita (then six years old) go away to kindergarten for the first time, and at the end of the day come back crying because she hadn't known the answers to some of the questions the teacher asked her.

Nita's crying had upset Dairine more than anything else in her short life. It had instantly become plain to Dairine's three-year-old mind that the world was a dangerous place if you didn't know things, a place that would make you unhappy if it could. Right there she decided that she was not going to be one of the unhappy ones.

So she got smart. She started out by working to keep her ears and eyes open, noticing everything; not surprisingly, Dairine's senses became abnormally sharp, and stayed that way. She found out how to read by the time she was four . . . just how, she never remembered: but at five she was already working her way through the encyclopedias her parents had bought for Nita. The first time they caught her at it—reading aloud to herself from a *Britannica* article on taxonomy, and sounding out the longer words—her mom and dad were shocked, though for a long time Dairine couldn't understand why. It had never occurred to her that you could use what you knew, use even the knowing itself, to make people feel things . . . perhaps even to make them do things.

For fear of her parents being upset, and maybe stopping her, until she was six or so she kept her reading out of their sight as much as she could. The thought of being kept away from books terrified her. Most of what moved Dairine was sheer delight of learning, the great openness of the world that reading offered her, even though she herself wasn't free to explore the world yet. But there was also that obscure certainty, buried under the months and years since the decision, that the sure way to make the world work for you was to know everything. Dairine sat home and busied herself with conquering the world.

Eventually it came time for her to go off to kindergarten. Remembering Nita, her parents were braced for the worst, but not at all for Dairine's scowling, annoyed response when she came home. "They won't listen to what I tell them," Dairine said. *"Yet."* And off she went to read, leaving her mother and father staring at each other.

School went on, and time, and Dairine sailed her way up through the grades. She knew (having overheard a couple of her mother's phone conversations with the school's psychiatrist) that her parents had refused to let her skip grades. They thought it would be better for her to be with kids of her own age. Dairine laughed to herself over this, since it made school life utterly easy for her: it also left her more free time for her own pursuits, especially reading. As soon as she was old enough to go to the little local library for herself, she read everything in it: first going straight through the kids' library downstairs at about six books a day, then (after the concerned librarian got permission from Dairine's parents) reading the whole adult collection, a touch more slowly. Her mom and dad thought it would be a shame to stifle such an active curiosity. Dairine considered this opinion wise, and kept reading, trying not to think of the time—not too far away—when she would exhaust the adult books. She wasn't yet allowed to go to the big township library by herself.

But she had her dreams, too. Nita was already being allowed to go into New York City alone. In a few years, she would too. Dairine thought constantly of the New York Public Library, of eight million books that the White Lions guarded: rare manuscripts, books as old as printing, or older. It would take even Dairine a while to get through eight million books. She longed to get started.

And there were other dreams more immediate. Like everyone else she knew, Dairine had seen the Star Wars movies. Magic, great power for good and evil, she had read about in many other places. But the Star Wars movies somehow hit her with a terrible immediacy that the books had not; with a picture of power available even to untrained farmboys on distant planets in the future, and therefore surely available to someone who knew things in the present. And if you could learn that supreme knowledge, and master the power that filled and shaped the universe, how could the world ever hurt you? For a while Dairine's reading suffered, and her daydreams were full of the singing blaze of lightsabers, the electric smell of blasterfire, and the shadow of ultimate evil in a black cloak, which after terrible combat she always defeated. Her sister teased her a lot less about it than Dairine expected.

Her sister. . . . Their relationship was rather casual, not so much a relative-relationship as the kind you might have with someone who lived close enough for you to see every day. When both Dairine and Nita were little, they had played to-

★ 18 ★

gether often enough. But where learning came in, for a while there had been trouble. Sometimes Nita had shown Dairine things she was learning at school. But when Dairine learned them almost immediately, and shortly was better at them than Nita was, Nita got upset. Dairine never quite understood why. It was a victory for them both, wasn't it, over the world, which would get you if you didn't know things? But Nita seemed not to understand that.

Eventually things got better. As they got older, they began to grow together and to share more. Possibly Nita was understanding her better, or had simply seen how much Dairine liked to know things; for she began to tutor Dairine in the upper-grade subjects she was studying, algebra and so forth. Dairine began to like her sister. When they started having trouble with bullies, and their parents sent them both off to self-defense school, Dairine mastered that art as quickly as anything else she'd ever decided to learn; and then, when a particularly bad beating near home made it plain that Nita wasn't using what they'd learned, she quietly put the word out that anyone who messed with Nita would have Dairine to deal with. The bullying stopped, for both of them, and Dairine felt smugly satisfied.

That is, she did until one day after school she saw a kid come at Nita to "accidentally" body-block her into the dirt of the playground she was crossing. Dairine started to move to prevent it—but as the kid threw himself at Nita, he abruptly slid sideways off the air around her as if he had run into a glass wall. No one else seemed to notice. Even the attacker looked blank as he fell sideways into the dust. But Nita smiled a little, and kept on walking . . . and suddenly the world fell out from under Dairine, and everything was terribly wrong. *Her sister knew something she didn't.*

Dairine blazed up in a raging fire of curiosity. She began watching Nita closely, and her best friend, Kit, too, on a hunch. Slowly Dairine began to catch Nita at things no one else seemed to notice; odd words muttered to empty air, after which lost things abruptly became found, or stuck things came loose.

There was one day when their father had been complaining about the crabgrass in the front lawn, and Dairine had seen an odd, thoughtful look cross Nita's face. That evening her sister had sat on the lawn for a long time, talking under her breath. Dairine couldn't hear what was said; but a week and a half later their father was standing on and admiring a crabgrass-free lawn, extolling the new brand of weedkiller he'd tried. He didn't notice, as Dairine did, the large patch of crabgrass under the apple trees in the neighbor's yard next door . . . carpeting a barren place where the neighbor had been trying to get something green to grow, anything, for as long as Dairine could remember. It was all stuff like that . . . little things, strange things, nothing Dairine could understand and use.

Then came summer vacation at the beach—and the strangeness started to come out in the open. Nita and Kit started spending a lot of time away from home, sneaking in and out as if there were something to hide. Dairine heard her mother's uneasy conversations about this with her father, and was amused; whatever Nita was doing with Kit, Dairine knew sex wasn't involved. Dairine covered for Nita and Kit, and bided her time, waiting until they should owe her something.

The time came soon enough. One night the two of them went swimming and didn't come back when it got dark, as they'd agreed to. Dairine's mom and dad went out looking for Nita and Kit on the beach, and took Dairine with them. She got separated from them, mostly on purpose, and was a quarter-mile down the beach from them when, with a rush of water and noisy breath, a forty-foot humpback whale breached right in front of her, ran itself aground—and turned into Nita.

Nita went white with shock at the sight of Dairine. Dairine didn't care. "You're going to tell me *everything*," she said, and ran down the beach to distract her parents just long enough for Nita and Kit—also just changed back from a whale—to get back into their bathing suits. And after the noisy, angry scene with their parents that followed, after the house was quiet, Dairine went to Nita's

★ 21 ★

room, where Kit was waiting, too, and let them tell her the whole story.

Wizards' manuals, oaths, wizardry, spells, quests, terrible dangers beyond the world, great powers that moved unseen and unsuspected beneath the surface of everyday existence, and every now and then broke surface—Dairine was ecstatic. It was all there, everything she had longed for. And if they could have it, she could have it too. . . .

Dairine saw their faces fall, and felt the soft laughter of the world starting behind her back again. You couldn't have this magic unless you were offered it by the Powers that controlled it. Yes, sometimes it ran in families, but there was no guarantee that it would ever pass to you. . . .

At that point Dairine began to shut their words out. She promised to keep their secret for the time being, and to cover for them the best she could. But inside she was all one great frustrated cry of rage: *Why them, why them and not me!* Days later, when the cry ebbed, the frustration gave way to blunt, stubborn determination. *I'll have it. I will.*

She had gone into Nita's room, found her wizard's manual, and opened it. The last time she'd held it it had looked like a well-worn kid's book from the library and, when she'd borrowed it, had read like one. Now the excitement, the exultation, flared up in Dairine again; for instead of a story she found pages and pages of an Arabic-looking

★ 22 ★

script she couldn't read . . . and near the front, many that she could, in English.

She skimmed them, turning pages swiftly. The pages were full of warnings and cautions, phrases about the wizard's responsibility to help slow down the death of the universe, paragraphs about the price each wizard paid for his new power, and about the terrible Ordeal-quest that lay before every novice who took the Wizards' Oath: sections about old strengths that moved among the worlds, not all of them friendly. But these Dairine scorned as she'd scorned Nita's cautions. The parts that spoke of a limitless universe full of life and of wizards to guard it, of "the Billion Homeworlds," "the hundred million species of humanity," those parts stayed with her, filled her mind with images of strangeness and glory and adventure until she was drowning in her own thought of unnumbered stars. I can do it, she thought. I can take care of myself. I'm not afraid. I'll matter, I'll *be* something. . . .

She flipped through the English section to its end, finding there one page, with a single block of type set small and neat.

In Life's name, and for Life's sake, I assert that I will employ the Art which is Its gift in Life's service alone. I will guard growth and ease pain. I will fight to preserve what grows and lives well in its own way; nor will I change any creature unless its growth and life, or that of the system of which it is part, are threatened. To these ends, in the practice of my Art, I will ever put aside fear for courage, and death for life, when it is fit to do so—looking always toward the Heart of Time, where all our sundered times are one, and all our myriad worlds lie whole, in That from Which they proceeded. . . .

It was the Oath that Nita had told her about. Not caring that she didn't understand parts of it, Dairine drew a long breath and read it out loud, almost in triumph. And the terrible silence that drew itself down around her as she spoke, blocking out the sounds of day, didn't frighten her; it exhilarated her. Something was going to happen, at last, at last. . . .

She went to bed eagerly that night.

Up and Running

Nita and Kit and Dairine made their way among the shops of the lower level of Penn Station and caught the C train for the Upper West Side, coming up at Eighty-first and Central Park West. For a little bit they stood there just getting their bearings. It was warm, but not uncomfortable yet. The park glowed green and golden.

Dairine was fidgeting. "Now where?"

"Right here," Nita said, turning around. The four-block stretch behind them, between 77th and 81st streets, was commanded by the huge, graceful bulk of the American Museum of Natural History, with its marble steps and beast-carved pediment, and the great bronze equestrian statue of Teddy Roosevelt looking eastward across at the park.

Tucked into a corner of the building on 81st Street stood the art deco–looking brick cube of the Hayden Planetarium, topped with a greened-copper dome.

"It looks like a tomb," Dairine said. "Shove *that*. I'm going to Natural History and look at the stuffed elephants."

"Climb on the stuffed elephants, you mean," Nita said. "Forget it. You're staying with us."

"Oh? What makes you think you can keep track of me if I decide to—"

"This," Kit said grimly, hefting his wizard's manual. "If we have to, we can put a tracer on you. Or a leash . . ."

"Oh, yeah? Well, listen, smart guy, *I*—"

"Kit," Nita said under her breath, "easy. Dari, are you out of your mind? This place is full of *space* stuff. The new Shuttle mock-up. A meteorite ten feet long." She smiled slightly. "A store with Star Wars books . . ."

Dairine stared at Nita. "Well, why didn't you say so? Come on." She headed down the cobblestone driveway toward the planetarium doors.

"You never catch that fly with vinegar," Nita said quietly to Kit as the two of them followed at a safe distance.

"She's not like my sisters," Kit said.

"Yeah. Well, your sisters are human beings. . . ."

They snickered together and went in after Dairine. To Nita's mild relief—because paying for her little sister's ticket would have killed her hot-dog money—Dairine already had admission money with her. "Dad give you that?" Nita said as she paid.

"No, this is mine," said Dairine, wrapping the change up with the rest of a wad, and sticking it back in her shorts.

"Where'd you get all that?"

"I taught a couple guys in my class to play poker last month," said Dairine. And off she went, heading for the souvenir store.

"Neets?" Kit said, tossing his manual in one hand.

Nita thought about it. "Naah," she said. "Let her go. Dairine!"

"What?"

"Just don't leave the building!"

"Okay."

"Is that safe?" Kit said.

"What, leaving her alone? She'll get into the Shuttle mock-up and not come out till closing time. Good thing there's hardly anyone here. Besides, she did say she wouldn't leave. If she were going to weasel out of it, she would've just grunted or something."

The two of them paused to glance into the souvenir store, full of books and posters and T-shirts and hanging *Enterprise*s—both shuttle and starship. Dairine was browsing through a *Return of the Jedi* picture book. "Whatcha gonna get, hotshot?" Kit said, teasing.

"Dunno." She put the book down. "What I really need," she said, looking down at a set of Apollo decals, "is a lightsaber."

"And what would you do with it once you had it?"

"Use it on Darth Vader," Dairine said. "Don't you two have somewhere to be?"

Nita considered the image of Dairine facing down Darth Vader, lightsaber in hand, and felt sorry for Vader. "C'mon," she said to Kit. They ambled down the hall a little way, to the Ahnighito meteorite on its low pedestal—thirty-four tons of nickel–iron slag, pitted with great holes like an irregularly melted lump of Swiss cheese. Nita laid her hands and cheek against it; on a hot day in New York, this was the best thing in the city to touch, for its pleasant coolness never altered, no matter how long you were in contact with it. Kit reached out and touched it too.

"This came a long way," he said.

"The asteroid belt," Nita said. "Two hundred fifty million miles or so . . ."

"No," Kit said. "Farther than that." His voice was quiet, and Nita realized that Kit was deep in the kind of wizardly "understanding" with the meteorite that she had with trees and animals and other things that lived. "Long, long dark times," Kit said, "nothing but space, and the cold. And then slowly, light growing. Faster and faster—diving in toward the light, till it burns, and gas and water and metal boil off one after another. And before everything's gone, out into the dark again, for a long, long time. . . ."

"It was part of a comet," Nita said.

"Until the comet's orbit decayed. It came in too close to the Sun on one pass, and shattered, and came down—" Kit took his hand away abruptly. "It doesn't care for that memory," he said.

"And now here it is. . . ."

"Tamed," Kit said. "Resting. But it remembers when it was wild, and roamed in the dark, and the Sun was its only tether. . . ."

Nita was still for a few seconds. That sense of the Earth being a small safe "house" with a huge backyard, through which powers both benign and terrible moved, was what had first made her fall in love with astronomy. To have someone share the feeling with her so completely was amazing. She met Kit's eyes, and couldn't think of anything to say; just nodded.

"When's the sky show?" he said.

"Fifteen minutes."

"Let's go."

They spent the afternoon drifting from exhibit to exhibit, playing with the ones that wanted playing with, enjoying themselves and taking their time. To

Nita's gratification, Dairine stayed mostly out of their way. She did attach herself to them for the sky show, which may have been lucky; for Dairine got fascinated by the big Zeiss star projector, standing under the dome like a giant lens-studded dumbbell, and only threats of violence kept her out of the open booth that contained the computer-driven controls.

When the sky show was done, Dairine went off to the planetarium store to add a few more books to the several she'd already bought. Nita didn't see her again until late in the afternoon, when she and Kit were trying out the scales that told you your weight on various planets. Nita had just gotten on the scale for Jupiter, which weighed her in at twenty-one hundred pounds.

"Putting on a little weight, there, Neets," Dairine said behind her. "Especially up front."

Nita almost turned around and decked her sister. Their mom had just taken Nita to buy her first bra, and her feelings about this were decidedly mixed— a kind of pride combined with embarrassment, because none of the girls she hung out with had one yet, and she had become the focus of some slight envy. It all made her uncomfortable, and Dairine, sensing this, had been running the subject into the ground for days.

She can stuff it right up!, Nita thought fiercely, I am not going to let her get to me! "All muscle,

Dair," she said. "Besides, it's where you are that counts. Check this out." She sidestepped to the Mars scale, the needle of which stopped at seven pounds. "Less than the Moon, even."

"But it's bigger than the Moon," Dairine said.

"But not as dense. That's why its atmosphere's so thin even though Mars is that big; its mass is too small to hold it—" Nita heard footsteps, turned around, and saw that she had lost her audience. "Dairine? Where you headed?"

"Bathroom." Dairine's voice came from halfway down the stairs to the lower level.

"Well, hurry up, it's almost closing time."

Kit, on the Saturn scale, moved over to the Jupiter. "What was that all about?" he said. "I don't often hear you think these days, but if your dad had heard your mind right after she said that, he would've washed your head out with soap."

"Oh, crap." She tried the scale for Mercury: three and a half pounds. "I'm growing."

"You don't look any taller."

"Kit!"

"Oh." He looked at her chest. "Oh. I guess." He shrugged. "I didn't notice."

Oh, thank heaven, Nita thought, and immediately after that, He didn't notice? She swallowed and said, "Anyway, she's been riding me. I'm gonna kill her if she keeps it up."

"Maybe she's jealous."

Nita laughed. "Her? Of *me?*"

"Sure." Kit got off the scales and began to pace off the space between the scales and the doors to the planetarium proper. "Neets, wake up. You're a wizard. Here Dairine's been hot for magic since she was a little kid—any kind, Star Wars, you name it—and all of a sudden, not only does it turn out that there really *is* such a thing, but *you* turn up with it. From what you had to tell her to keep her quiet after she found out, Dari knows that you and I do big stuff. She wishes she could get her hands on the power. And there's no guarantee she ever will."

"She was into my manual over the last couple of days, I think. . . ."

"So there you are. If she can't have the magic, she's gonna twist you around whatever other way she can. I hate to say this, Neets, but she's a real brat."

That agreed too well with thoughts Nita had been having, but had rejected. "Well. . . ."

"Ladies and gentlemen," said a woman's voice from the ceiling speakers down the hall, "the planetarium is now closing. Thank you."

Nita sighed. Kit punched her lightly in the arm. "Come on," he said, "don't let her get you down. Let's go over to the park and get hot dogs. She starts getting on our nerves, we'll tell her we'll turn her into a fire hydrant and call in every dog in Manhattan to try her out."

★ 32 ★

"Too late," Nita said. "She already knows we don't do that kind of thing."

"She knows *you* don't do that kind of thing," Kit said. "She doesn't know that *I* don't. . . ."

Nita looked at his grim expression and wondered briefly whether the grimness was all faked. "I *am* starved."

"So c'mon."

They headed down the stairs together and came out on the ground floor, by the front doors. In the stairwell, under an arrow pointing toward the basement level, was a sign they had seen earlier that day, and laughed at:

TO MARS, VENUS, AND LADIES' ROOM

"Wait for me," Nita said. "She's probably trying to break into that Venus exhibit to see where the 'lava' comes from."

Kit rolled his eyes. "Being a fire hydrant may be too good for her."

Nita went down the stairs. "Dari?" she called, annoyed. "Come on before they lock us in."

It was considerably cooler down here. Nita turned right at the bottom of the stairs and walked quickly through the Venus exhibit, rubbing her upper arms at the chill, which went right through her thin T-shirt. Someone had turned off the sluggishly erupting Venerian volcano behind its murky glass wall; no one was to be seen anywhere else, all the way down to the temporary plasterboard wall with the sign that said MARS CLOSED FOR RENOVATIONS.

"Don't tell me she's still *in* the toilet," Nita muttered, annoyed. Reading, probably. One of these days she's gonna fall in. She went back the way she had come, past the stairs, to the ladies' room. It was not only cold down here, there was a draft. She grabbed the handle of the door and pulled; it resisted her slightly, and there was a faint *hoo* noise, air sliding through the door crack as she tugged. "Dari? Come on, we're leaving!" Nita pulled harder, the door came open—

Air blew hard past her and ruffled her hair into her eyes. Bitter cold smote the front of her, and in it the humidity in the air condensed out instantly, whipping past Nita through the sucking air as stinging, dust-fine snow.

Nita was looking through the doorway into a low rust-red wasteland: nothing but stones in all sizes, cracked, tumbled, piled, with dun dust blowing between them. Close, much too close to be normal, lay a horizon hazed in blood-brown, shading up through translucent brick color, rose, violet, a hard dark blue, and above everything, black with stars showing. Low in the crystalline rose burned a small pinkish sun, fierce, distant-looking, and cold. Nita flinched from the unsoftened sight of it, from the long, harsh shadows it laid out behind every smallest stone. She slammed the ladies' room door shut. Air kept moaning past her, through the cracks, out into the dry red wasteland.

"Mars," she breathed, and terror grabbed her heart and squeezed. "She went to *Mars*. . . !"

Escape Key

That morning Dairine had awakened with the Oath's words ringing in her ears to find herself not in a galaxy far far away, but in her own bed. She had lain there for a long few minutes in bitter annoyance before she heard the wheels of the truck in the driveway. It was the computer, of course: and to this lesser excitement she had gratefully surrendered herself.

Dairine was good with computers. It was just one more kind of knowledge, good for using to keep people and the World off your back; and computers were really surprisingly easy to work with once you got it through your head that they were utterly stupid things, unable to do anything you didn't tell them how to do, in language they understood. In her few months' work with the Apples at school, Dairine had become an accomplished hacker.

She utterly disdained the "phreaking," the breaking and entering of electronic bulletin boards and systems that interested a few of her malicious classmates. It could get you thrown in jail. What fascinated Dairine was advanced programming, the true hacking—getting a computer to sing, or talk, or play involved and clever games, or make you a sandwich. All these things were possible, with the right peripherals and a smart programmer. That she was; and the computer—tireless listener, absolutely obedient to orders, and endlessly forgiving of mistakes—was the perfect companion. They worked well together. Even her teachers had noticed that the machines "behaved" better around Dairine than around anyone else. She never noticed this herself, having taken it for granted.

So while her mother and father sat arguing over the manuals, of course Dairine took matters into her own hands. The Apple IIIc+ was easy to set up: a plug and cable for the screen, the printer cable attached to the printer port and the computer's interface; the power cord to the wall. Dairine slipped a system disk into the drive, shut the drive door, and turned the computer on, "booted it up"—ready to look for the "Copy" utility in the disk's directory. The first thing you always did with a brand-new system disk full of programs was copy it; working on the original disk could cost you a lot of money to replace if you hurt or wiped it accidentally.

The Apple logo came up on the screen, and below it the A> prompt that said the computer's basic operating system, called DOS, was ready to accept commands to its "A" or onboard disk drive and the disk inside it. Dairine was about to start typing when something about the logo caught her eye. It was the famous striped Apple, all right: but it had no bite out of it.

She stared for a second. Pirated software? she thought, but that was ridiculous. Her dad had bought the computer and its system software from an approved dealer, and the various warranties, manuals and end-user agreements were all over the floor. Huh. Maybe they changed the logo. Oh, well. Let's see the directory. . . .

DIR A: , she typed on the keyboard, and hit the carriage return.

PASSWORD? said the screen, and sat there apparently waiting for a response, for the A> prompt hadn't come back.

That was no response she'd ever seen on the machines at school. DIR A: , she typed, again, and the carriage return.

PASSWORD?

"Huh," she said to herself, as possibilities flickered through her head. Did Dad have the software encrypted somehow so that Nita and I can't get into it? But why? He wants us to use it. She let out a breath. Maybe it just wants an ID code for the user —there're some programs that do that. She squinted at the screen a moment, then smiled and typed in a private joke: the code name that a certain untrained farmboy used in his fighter run on the Death Star, a name that suited Dairine since she had inherited her mother's red hair. RED FIVE, she typed, and hit the carriage return.

PASSWORD RED FIVE ACCEPTED.

A>

Weird, Dairine thought, and typed again.

DIR A:

The disk drive whirred. The screen wiped itself and displayed a list: mostly program command files, or data files holding information for the programs, to judge by their suffixes.

ASSIST.COM	22008K
CHANGE.COM	2310K
COPY.COM	1032K
COPY.DAT	4404K
GO.COM	5048K
GO.DAT	3580K
HIDE.COM	1244K
MANUAL.COM	3248K
MANUAL.DAT	10662K
MBASIC.COM	7052K
MENU.COM	256K

```
SEEK.COM          6608K
SUPPORT.COM       5120K
SUPPORT.DAT       3218K
A>
```

Dairine gazed at the screen, perplexed. A *K* was a kilobyte, a thousand little pieces or bytes of information; and the disk drive itself was supposed to hold only 800 K. How could the disk possibly have all these files on it, and such big ones?

Maybe this is a bad disk, Dairine thought. It happened sometimes, that a disk was damaged on its way from the factory. Or maybe something was wrong with the directory. Well, let's see if something'll run. Beside the A> prompt she typed "COPY" and hit the carriage return.

The disk drive whirred. The screen wiped itself again, then said:

```
IIIC COPY UTILITY
5430K FREE
RADIUS?
```

Dairine stared again. *Radius* meant nothing to her. She hit the carriage return, hoping the computer would (as some programs did) supply its own data as a result.

DEFAULT RADIUS, the screen said. It was all right, then; the program had been instructed to supply a value of its own if the user didn't specify one.

★ 41 ★

Dairine let out a breath, and resolved to have a look at this thing's manual. Maybe the company had made changes in the software.

COPY UTILITY READY, said the screen. PRESS <CR> TO BEGIN.

Dairine hit the carriage return. The disk drive whirred.

There were two computers on the desk.

She gaped. Hesitantly she put out a hand to the second computer, which was sitting next to the first, and sticking over the edge of the desk a little. It was solid, and its screen matched that of the original computer exactly. They both said:

COPY SUCCESSFULLY COMPLETED.
DESCRIPTION FILE "APPLIIIC.DSC" CREATED
HARD COPY "APPLIIIC.CPY" CREATED

A>

Oh, Lord! Dairine thought. She didn't dare turn around or make any outward sign: behind her, her mother and father were arguing peaceably over the contents of the Apple manuals. Desperately, Dairine brought up the directory again, stared at it, and then, for lack of any better idea, typed:

HIDE

The disk drives whirred again. Dairine thought she had never heard such a loud noise in her life,

but her parents still didn't notice anything. The
screen cleared itself, then said:

IIIC HIDE UTILITY
Choose one:
(1) Hide from COPY utility
(2) Hide from CHANGE utility
(3) Hide from MBASIC
(4) Exit to system

Dairine typed "1." The screen cleared again.

HIDE FROM "COPY" UTILITY

Last copy description file in
memory: "APPLIIIC.DSK"

Last hard copy created: "APPLIIIC.CPY"

Name of hard copy to
hide?

Dairine hurriedly typed "APPLIII.CPY." The
screen said:

HIDE OPTIONS:
(a) Hide in realspace
     (invisibility option)
(b) Hide in realspace
     (size reduction)
(c) Hide in otherspace
     (retrievable pocket)

(d) Discard in otherspace
     (nonretrievable pocket)

(e) Timed storage
     (coordinate-specific claudication)

(f) Exit to main menu

Dairine typed "c."

PASSWORD FOR RETRIEVAL?

Dairine swallowed: behind her, her father was muttering about getting some coffee. "RED FIVE," she typed.

CHOOSE INPUT OPTION: VERBAL OR KEYBOARD?

"VERBAL," she typed, very fast.
The drives whirred.

HIDING HARD COPY OF FILE "APPLIIIC.CPY."

As silently as it had come, the second computer vanished.

A>

Dairine's father turned around and saw her at the computer. *"What are you doing!"*

"Uh," Dairine said. She couldn't remember when she had last been at a loss for words. Her father, though, wasn't even slightly concerned with this.

Several seconds later Dairine found herself going to New York with Nita and Kit.

At the moment, even the thought of the New York Public Library seemed a bit tame.

It took her hours to get free of Nita and Kit. All the while her mind was raging, turning over and over the thought of what power she had been offered when she took the Oath, and when she finally got down to the ladies' room and sat down in one of the stalls, her heart was hammering with excitement and sweat stood out on her.

"Red five," she whispered, and held her breath.

There was a computer in her lap.

She flipped up the little liquid-crystal screen and was shocked to find the A> prompt staring at her: shocked partly because she hadn't booted the computer up, and partly because it couldn't be running —there were no batteries in it yet—or were there? But Dairine wasn't one to argue the point. She typed hurriedly, using the HIDE.COM program to put the books she'd bought in a "pocket" and get them out of her way. Then she brought up the directory again. ASSIST.COM, said the first entry. Maybe that was a "help menu," a series of screens that would explain how to get the most out of the computer. She typed "ASSIST" and the carriage return.

The screen cleared, then said at the top:

Dairine was out of her depth again. "ACTIVE," she typed, on a guess, and entered it. The screen cleared again.

UTILITY OPTIONS:

(1)   General Data & Logistics—MANUAL, MENU

(2)   Travel—GO.COM

(3)   Intervention—CHANGE (see also MAN-UAL)

(3a)   Duplication—COPY

(3b)   Preservation—HIDE, SEEK

(4)   Outside assistance—(routine) SUPPORT

(4a)   (emergency) ASSIST

(5)   Other programming—MBASIC

(6)   Exit to system

Dairine chewed her lip and thought. Just to see what would happen, she hit "2" and the carriage return. The screen cleared.

TRAVEL UTILITY

Input? (1) keyboard, (2) verbal

"2," Dairine typed.

"Inside solar system or outside solar system?"

★ 46 ★

the computer said very quietly, but so suddenly that Dairine almost dropped it.

"Inside," she said, and swallowed.

"Planet?"

She gazed at the ladies' room door, thinking of the dioramas outside with a sudden terrible desire. "Mars," Dairine said.

The disk drive chirred briefly. "Coordinates?"

Dairine knew that aerographers used some kind of latitude–longitude system for Mars, but she knew nothing else about it. "Default," she said, on a hunch.

"Default coordinates confirmed," said the computer, "last recorded transit. Atmosphere?"

Last recorded— "Uh, atmosphere? Yes," she said.

"Parameters?"

"Umm. . . . Fifteen percent oxygen, eighty percent nitrogen, five percent carbon dioxide."

"Mix proportions approximate Terran sea-level parameters. Default to those?"

"Mmm . . . Yes."

"Estimated time in transit?"

She thought. "One hour."

"Data complete," said the computer. "Ready to transit. Transit command 'run.'"

"Run," Dairine said.

And everything slewed sideways and upside down. Or no, the world stayed the same—but Dairine's frame of reference suddenly became huger than the whole Earth and the space that con-

★ 47 ★

tained it, so that her planet seemed only one moving, whirling point plunging along its path through a terrible complexity of forces, among which gravity was a puny local thing and not to be regarded. Up was some other way now; down had nothing to do with the floor. Her stomach rebelled.

And her eyes were seeing things they had never been made to see. Lines and sparks and traces of white fire seemed to tear through her head from her eyes to the back of her skull; they pinned her to the rolling Earth like a feebly fluttering moth to a card. A terrible silence with a deadly sea-roar at the bottom of it, more terrible than the stillness of her Oathtaking, flattened her down with its sheer cold ancientness, a vast weight of years without sound or light or life. Cosmic rays, she thought desperately, clutching at reason: faster-than-light particles, maybe that's what the light is. But the dark—it's death, death itself, I'm going to die—

—and the wizardry let her go. Dairine got shakily to her feet. The first crunch of stones and gravel under her sneakers, instead of tile floor, went through her in a rush of adrenaline as fierce as fire. Her vision cleared. Red wasteland stretched away under a cold rose sun, a violet sky arched over her; the wind sang chill. She turned slowly, looking around. High up in the cold violet day, something small and bright fled across the sky, changing phase as it did so.

"Deimos," Dairine whispered. Or maybe it was

Phobos, the other of Mars's two little moons. Whichever it was, it went through half its month in a few minutes, sliding down toward the horizon and down behind something that stood up from it. It was a mountain peak, upraised as if on a pedestal, and so tall that though it came up from far behind the foreshortened horizon, its broad flat base spanned half that horizon easily. "What is that?" she said.

"Syntax error 24," said the Apple dispassionately. "Rephrase for precision."

"That mountain. What is it? Identify."

"Earth/IAU nomenclature 'Olympus Mons.'"

Dairine took in a sharp breath. It was an ancient volcano, long extinct, and the highest mountain in the Solar System. "How do I get up there?"

"Reference short-transit utilities."

She did. Five minutes later she stood in a place where the wind no longer sang, for it was too thin to do so; where carbon dioxide lay frozen on the rust-red stones, and the fringes of her protective shell of air shed a constant snow of dry ice and water vapor as she moved; a place from which she could see the curvature of the world. Dairine stood twelve miles high atop Olympus Mons, on the ridge of its great crater, into which Central Park could have been dropped entire, and looked out over the curve of the red world at what no nonwizardly child of Earth had seen with her or his own eyes before: the asteroid belt rising like a chain of scattered stars, and beyond them, the tiniest possible disk, remote but clear.

"Jupiter," she whispered, and turned around to look for Earth. From here it would look like a morning or evening star, just a shade less bright than Venus. But in mid-movement she was distracted. There was something down in the mile-deep crater, a little light that shone.

"What's that?" she said, holding up the Apple.

"Syntax error 24—"

"Yeah, yeah, right. That light! Identify."

"A marker beacon. Provenance uncertain at this range."

"Get us down there!"

With Dairine's help, it did. Shortly she was staring at a pole with a light on it, streamlined and modern-looking, made of some dark blue metal she couldn't identify. Set in the ground beside the pole was a plate of dull red metal with strange markings on it. "What's it say?"

"Error trap 18. Sense of query: semantic value?"

"Right."

"First (untranslatable) climbing expedition. Ascent of (untranslatable proper name): from (date uncertain) to (date uncertain). We were here. Signed, (untranslatable proper name), (untranslatable proper name), (untranslatable proper name)."

"People," Dairine whispered.

"Affirmative."

She looked up at the stars in the hard violet sky. "I want to go where they came from!"

"Reference transit utility."

She did, and spent some minutes tapping busily at the keys. In the middle of it, selecting coordinates, delightedly reading through planet names— she stopped and bit her lip. "This is going to take longer than an hour," she said to herself. Come to think of it, she might want to be away for quite some time. And seeing all the problems Nita had started having with their folks when she told them she was a wizard, it wouldn't do for Dairine to let them know that she was one too. Not just yet.

She thought about this, then got out of the "travel" utility and brought up the directory again —taking more time with it, examining the program menus with great care. In particular she spent a great deal of time with the "Copy" and "Hide" utilities, getting to know their ins and outs, and doing one finicky piece of copying as a test. The test worked: she sent the copy home.

"That should do it," she said, got back into the "Travel" utility, and with the program's prompting started to lay in coordinates. "Darth Vader," she muttered under her breath, "look out. Here I come."

Shortly thereafter there was nothing on Olympus Mons but rocks, and dry-ice snow, and far down in the crater, the single blinking light.

Search and Retrieval

"We're dead," Nita mourned, sitting on the planetarium steps with her head in her hands. "Dead. My mother will kill me."

Kit, sitting beside her, looked more bemused than upset. "Do you know how much power it takes to open a gateway like that and leave it open? Usually it's all we can do to keep one open long enough to jump through it."

"Big deal! Grand Central gate and the World Trade Center portals are open all the time." Nita groaned again. *"Mars!"*

"Each of those gates took a hundred or so wizards working together to open, though." Kit leaned back on the steps. "She may be a brat, but boy, has she got firepower!"

"The youngest wizards always do," Nita said, sitting up again and picking up Kit's manual from beside her. "Lord, what a horrible thought."

"What? The gate she made? We can close it, but—"

"No. This. Look." She held out his manual. It was turned to one of the directory pages. The page said:

CALLAHAN, Juanita T.   Journeyman rating
243 E. Clinton Avenue   (RL +4.5 +/− .15)
Hempstead NY 11575   Available/limited
(516) 555-6786   (summer vacation)

That was Nita's usual directory listing, and normal enough. But above it, between her and CAHANE, Jak, whose listing was usually right above hers, there was something new.

CALLAHAN, Dairine E.   Novice rating
243 E. Clinton Avenue   (RL +9.8 +/− .2)
Hempstead NY 11575   on Ordeal: no calls
(516) 555-6786

"Oh, no," Kit said. "And look at that rating level."

Nita dropped the book beside her. "I don't get it. She didn't find a manual, how could she have—"

"She was in yours," Kit said.

"Yeah, but the most she could have done was take the Oath! She's smart, but not smart enough to pull off a forty-million-mile transit without having the reference diagrams and the words for the spell

★ 54 ★

in front of her! And the manuals can't be stolen; you know that. They just vanish if someone tries." Nita put her head down in her hands again. "My folks are gonna pitch a fit! We've got to find her!"

Kit breathed out, then stood up. "Come on," he said. "We'd better start doing things fast or we'll lose her. There's a phone over there. Call home and tell them we're running a little behind schedule. The planetarium's all locked up by now: so no one'll be around to notice if I walk through a couple of walls and close that gate down."

"But what if she tries to come back and finds it closed behind her?"

"Somehow I can't see that slowing her down much," Kit said. "And besides, maybe she's supposed to find it closed. She *is* on Ordeal."

Nita stood up too. "And we'd better call Tom and Carl. They'll want the details."

"Right. Go ahead; I'll take care of the gate."

Kit turned around, looked at the bricks of the planetarium's outer wall. He stepped around the corner of the doorway wall, out of sight of the street, and laid one hand on the bricks, muttering under his breath. His hand sank into the wall as if into water. "There we go," he said, and the bricks rippled as he stepped through them and vanished.

Nita headed for the phone, feeling through her pockets for change. The thought of her sister running around the universe on Ordeal made her hair stand up on end. No one became a wizard without there being some one problem that their acquisition of power would solve. Nita understood from her studies that normally a wizard was allowed to get as old as possible before being offered the Oath: the Powers, her manual said, wanted every wizard who could to acquire the security and experience that a normal childhood provides. But sometimes, when problems of an unusual nature came up, the Powers would offer the Oath early—because the younger children, not knowing (or caring) what was impossible, had more wizardry available to them.

That kind of problem was likely to be a killer. Nita's Ordeal and Kit's had thrown them out of their universe into another one, a place implacably hostile to human beings, and run by the Power that, according to the manual, had invented death before time began—and therefore had been cast out of the other Powers' society. Every world had stories of that Lone Power, under many names. Nita didn't need the stories; she had met It face-to-face, twice now, and both times only luck—or the intervention of others—had saved her life. And Nita had been offered her wizardry relatively early, at thirteen: Kit even earlier, at twelve. The thought of what problem the Powers must need solved if They were willing to offer the Oath to someone years younger—and the thought of her little sister in the middle of it—

Nita found some quarters, went to a phone and

punched in her number. What was she going to tell her mother? She couldn't lie to her: that decision, made at the beginning of the summer, had caused her to tell her folks that she was a wizard, and had produced one of the great family arguments of her life. Her mother and father still weren't pleased that their daughter might run off anywhere at a moment's notice, to places where they couldn't keep an eye on her and protect her. Nor did it matter that those places tended to be the sort where anyone but an experienced wizard would quickly get killed. That made it even worse. . . .

At the other end, the phone rang. Nita's throat seized up. She began clearing it frantically.

Someone answered. "Hello?"

It was Dairine.

Nita's throat unseized itself. "Are you all right? Where are you?" she blurted, and then began swearing inwardly at her own stupidity.

"I'm fine," Dairine said. "And I'm right here."

"How did you get back? Never mind that, how did you get out? And you left the gate open! Do you know what could have happened if some poor janitor went in that door without looking? It's sixty below this time of year on Mars—"

"Nita," Dairine said, "you're babbling. Just go home. I'll see you later." And she hung up.

"Why that rotten little—" Nita said, and hung up the phone so hard that people on the street corner turned to look at her. Embarrassed and more annoyed than ever, she turned and headed back to where Kit was sitting. "Babbling," she muttered. "That rotten, thoughtless, I'm gonna—"

She shut her mouth. *Babbling?* That didn't sound like Dairine. It was too simple an insult. And why "just go home" instead of "just *come* home"? There's something wrong—

She stopped in front of Kit, who looked up at her from his seat on the step and made no move to get up. He was sweating and slightly pale. "That gate was fastened to Mars real tight," he said. "I thought half of Mariner Plain was going to come with it when I uprooted the forcefields. What's the matter with you? You look awful."

"Something's wrong," Nita said. "Dairine's home."

"What's awful about that? Good riddance." Then he looked at her sharply. "Wait a minute. Home? When she's on Ordeal?"

That hadn't even occurred to Nita. "She sounded weird," Nita said. "Kit, it didn't *sound* like her."

"We were at home for our Ordeal—at least, at the beginning . . ."

She shook her head. "Something's wrong. Kit, let's go see Tom and Carl."

He stood up, wobbling a little. "Sounds good. Grand Central?"

"Rockefeller Center gate's closer."

"Let's go."

* * *

A Senior wizard usually reaches that position through the most strenuous kind of training and field experience. All wizards, as they lose the power of their childhood and adolescence, tend to specialize in one field of wizardry or another; but the kind of wizard who's Senior material refuses to specialize too far. They are the Renaissance people of sorcery, every one of them tried repeatedly against the Lone Power, in both open combat and the subtler strife of one Power-influenced human mind against another. Seniors are almost never the white-bearded wizards of archetype . . . mostly because of their constant combats with the Lone One, which tend to kill them young. They advise other wizards on assignment, do research for them, lend them assistance in the losing battle to slow down the heat-death of the universe.

Few worlds have more than thirty or forty Seniors. At this point in Kit's and Nita's practice, Earth had twenty-four: six scattered through Asia, one in Australia and one (for the whales) in the Atlantic Ocean; three in Europe, four in Africa, and nine in the Americas—five in Central and South America (one of whom handled the Antarctic) and four in the north. Of these, one lived in Santa Cruz, one lived in Oklahoma City, and the other two lived together several miles away, in Nassau County.

Their house in Nita's town was very like their neighbors' houses . . . perhaps a little bigger, but that wasn't odd, since Carl worked as chief of sales for the big CBS flagship TV station in New York, and Tom was a moderately well-known freelance writer of stories and movie scripts. They looked like perfectly average people—two tall, good-looking men, one with a mustache, one without; Carl a native New Yorker, Tom an unrepentant Californian. They had all the things their neighbors had— mortgages and phone bills and pets and occasional fights: they mowed the lawn and went to work like everybody else (at least Carl did: Tom worked at home). But their lawn had as few weeds as Nita's did these days, their pets understood and sometimes spoke English and numerous other languages, their phone didn't always have a human being on the other end when it rang, and as for their fights, the reasons for some of them would have made their neighbors' mouths drop open.

Their backyard, being surrounded by a high hedge and a wall all hung with plants, was a safe place to appear out of nothing: though as usual there was nothing to be done about the small thundercrack of air suddenly displaced by two human bodies. When Nita's and Kit's ears stopped ringing, the first thing they heard was someone shouting, "All right, whatcha drop this time?" and an answering shout of "It wasn't me, are the dogs into something?" But they weren't: the two sheepdogs, Annie and Monty, came bounding out from around the corner of the house and leapt delightedly onto Kit and Nita, slurping any part of them not covered with clothes. A little behind them came Dudley the terrier, who contented himself with bouncing around them as if he were springloaded and barking at the top of his little lungs.

"Had dinner yet?" Carl called from the kitchen door, which, like the dining room doors, looked out on the backyard. "Annie! Monty! Down!"

"Bad dog! Bad dog! Nonono!" screamed another voice from the same direction: not surprising, since its source was sitting on Carl's shoulder. This was Machu Picchu the macaw, also known (to her annoyance) as "Peach": a splendid creature all scarlet and blue, with a three-foot tail, a foul temper, and a precognitive talent that could read the future for months ahead—if Peach felt like it. Wizards' pets tend to become strange with time, and Seniors' pets even stranger than usual; and Peach had been with them longer than any of the others. It showed.

"Come on in," called one last voice: Tom. Kit and Nita pushed Annie and Monty more or less back down to dog level, and made their way into the house through the dining room doors. It was a pleasant, open place, all the rooms running freely into one another, and full of handsome functional furniture: Tom's desk and computer sat in a comfortable corner of the living room. Kit pulled a chair away from the dining table and plopped down in it, still winded from his earlier wizardry.

Nita sat down next to him. Carl leaned over the table and pushed a pair of bottles of Coke at them, sitting down and cracking a third one himself. Tom, with a glass of iced coffee, sat down too.

"Hot one today," Carl said at last, putting his Coke down. Picchu sidled down his arm from his shoulder and began to gnaw thoughtfully on the neck of the bottle.

"No kidding," Kit said.

"You look awful," said Tom. "What've you two been up to?"

For answer Nita opened Kit's manual to the directory and pushed it over to Tom and Carl's side of the table. Tom read it, whistled softly, and nudged the manual toward Carl. "I saw this coming," he said, "but not this soon. Your mom and dad aren't going to be happy. Where did she go?"

"Mars," Kit said.

"Home," Nita said.

"Better start at the beginning," said Carl.

When they came to the part about the worldgate, Carl got up to go for his supervisory manual, and Tom looked at Kit with concern. "Better get him an aspirin too," Tom called after Carl.

"I'm allergic to aspirin."

"A Tylenol, then. You're going to need it. How did you manage to disalign a patent gateway all by yourself? . . . But wait a minute." Tom peered at Kit. "Are you taller than you were?"

"Two inches."

"That would explain it, then. It's a hormonal surge." Tom cleared his throat and looked at Nita. "You, too, huh?"

"Hormones? Yes. Unfortunately."

Tom raised his eyebrows. "Well. Your wizardry will be a little more accessible to you for a while than it has since you got started. Just be careful not to overextend yourself . . . it's easy to overreach your strength just now."

Carl came back with his supervisory manual, a volume thick as a phone book, and started paging through it. Annie nosed Kit from one side: he looked down in surprise and took the bottle of Tylenol she was carrying in her mouth. "Hey, thanks."

"Lord," Carl said. "She did a tertiary gating, all by herself. Your body becomes part of the gateway forcefields," he said, looking up at Nita and Kit. "It's one of the fastest and most effective kinds of gating, but it takes a lot of power."

"I still don't get it," Nita said. "She doesn't have a manual!"

"Are you sure?" Carl said; and "Have you gotten a computer recently?" said Tom.

"Just this morning."

Tom and Carl looked at each other. "I thought only Advisory levels and above were supposed to get the software version of the manual just yet," Carl said.

"Maybe, but she couldn't have stolen one of

those any more than she could have stolen one of the regular manuals. You're offered it . . . or you never see it."

Nita was puzzled. " 'Software version'?"

Tom gave her a wry look. "We've been beta-testing it," he said. "Sorry: testing the 'beta' version of the software, the one that'll be released after we're sure there are no bugs in it. You know the way you normally do spells? You draw your power diagrams and so forth as guides for the way you want the spell to work, but the actual instructions to the universe are spoken aloud in the Speech?"

"Uh-huh."

"And it takes a fair amount of practice to learn to do the vector diagrams and so forth without errors, and a lot of time, sometimes, to learn to speak the Speech properly. More time yet to learn to think in it. Well . . ." Tom sat down again and began turning his empty glass around and around on the table. "Now that technology has proceeded far enough on this planet for computers to be fairly widespread, the Powers have been working with the Senior wizards to develop computer-supported wizards' manuals. The software draws the necessary diagrams internally, the way a calculator does addition, for example; you get the solution without seeing how it's worked out. The computer also synthesizes the Speech, though of course there are tutorials in the language as you go along."

"The project has both useful and dangerous

sides," Carl said. "For one thing, there are good reasons why we use the Speech in spelling. It contains words that can accurately describe things and conditions that no Earthly language has words for. And if during a spell you give the computer instructions that're ambiguous in English, and it describes something inaccurately . . . well." He looked grim. "But for the experienced wizard, who already knows the theory he's working with, and is expert in the Speech, it can be a real timesaver."

"A lifesaver, too, under special circumstances," Tom said, looking somber. "You two know how many children go missing in this country every year."

"Thousands."

"It's not all kidnappings and runaways," Tom said. "Some of those kids are out on their Ordeal . . . and because they don't have time to become good with the Speech, they get in trouble with the Lone Power that they can't get out of. And they never come back." He moved uneasily in the chair. "Providing them with the wizard's software may save some of their lives. Meantime . . ."

Carl turned over a page or two in his manual, shaking his head. "Meantime, I want a look at Dairine's software; I need to see which version of it she got. And I want a word with her. If she lights out into the middle of nowhere on Ordeal without meaning the Oath she took, she's going to be in trouble up to her neck. . . . Anyway, your folks should know about all this. Easier if we tell them, I think. How 'bout it, partner?" He looked over at Tom.

"I was about to suggest it myself."

Nita sagged with relief.

"Good. Your folks busy this afternoon, Neets?"

"Just with the computer."

"Perfect." Carl put out his hand, and from the nearby kitchen wall the phone leapt into his hand. Or tried to: the phone cord brought it up short, and there it hung in the air, straining toward Carl like a dog at the end of a leash. "I thought you were going to put a longer cord on this thing," Carl said to Tom, pushing his chair back enough to get the phone up to his face, and hitting the autodialer in the handpiece. "This is ridiculous."

"The phone store was out of them again."

"Try that big hardware store down in Freeport, what's its name— Hi, Harry. Carl Romeo. . . . Nothing much, I just heard from Nita that you got the new computer. . . . Yeah, they stopped in on the way home. . . . Yeah. What did you decide on? . . . Oh, that's a sweet little machine. A lot of nice software for that." Carl listened for a few seconds to the soft squeaking of the phone, while Picchu left off chewing on Carl's Coke bottle and began nibbling delicately on the phone cord.

Carl smacked her gently away, and his eyebrows went up as he listened. "Okay. Fine. . . . Fine. See you in a bit. Bye now."

★ 66 ★

He hung up. "That was your mom in the background," he said to Nita, "insisting on feeding us again. I think she's decided the best thing to do with adult wizards is tame them with kindness and gourmet cuisine."

"Magic still makes her nervous," Nita said.

"Or we still make her nervous," Tom said, getting up to shut the doors.

"Well, yeah. Neither of them can quite get used to it, that you were their neighbors for all these years and they never suspected you were wizards. . . ."

"Being out in the open," Tom said, "causes even more problems than 'passing' . . . as you'll have noticed. But the truth works best. The front door locked?" he said to Carl.

"Yup," said Carl. He looked down at his side in surprise: from the table, Picchu was calmly climbing beak over claw up the side of his polo shirt. "Bird—"

"I'm going," said Picchu, achieving Carl's shoulder with a look of calm satisfaction, and staring Carl right in the eye. "I'm needed."

Carl shrugged. It was difficult and time-consuming to start fights with a creature who could rip your ear off faster than you could remove her. "You do anything nasty on their rug," he said, "and it's macaw croquettes for lunch tomorrow, *capeesh*?"

Picchu, preening a wing feather back into place, declined to answer.

★ 67 ★

"Then let's motor," Tom said. They headed for the garage.

"Lord," Tom said, "who writes these manuals, anyway? This is better than most, but it still might as well be in Sanskrit. Harry, where's that cable?" Nita watched with barely suppressed amusement as Tom and her father dug among the manuals all over the floor, and Tom went headfirst under the desk. "Computer seems to be running, anyway," Carl said.

"Had to drag Dairine away from it before she blew it up," said Mr. Callahan, peering under the desk to see what Tom was doing.

"Where is she, Daddy?" said Nita.

"In her room. You two must really have run her down for her to come home so early."

"Which train did she take?" Kit said.

"She didn't say. She looked a little tired when she got in . . . said she was going to go read or something. Tom, is that plug really supposed to go in there? It looks too big."

"They always do. See, this little bit inside the casing is all that actually goes in. Mmmf . . ."

Carl, standing beside Nita, reached around the back of the Apple and hit the reset button. The A> prompt that had been there vanished: the Apple logo came up again. It had no bite out of it.

Nita stared. "Uh huh," Carl said, and hit the CONTROL key and the letter C to boot up the system.

The A> prompt came back. Then Carl typed a string of numbers and figures, too quickly for them to register for Nita as anything but a green blur. They disappeared, and a message appeared in the graceful Arabic-looking letters of the wizardly Speech.

USER LOG?

"Yes, please," Carl said. "Authorization seven niner three seven one comma five one eight."

"Password?"

Carl leaned near the console and whispered something.

"Confirmed," said the computer politely, and began spilling its guts in screenful after screenful of green. "Pause," Carl said at one point. "Harry, I think you'd better have a look at this."

"What, did we plug it in wrong—"

"No, not that." Nita's father got up, brushing himself off, and looked at the screen. Then he froze. He had seen the Speech in Nita's manual once or twice, and knew the look of it.

"Carl," Nita's father said, beginning to look stern, "what is this?"

Carl looked as if he would rather not say anything. "Harry," he said, "it wouldn't be fair to make Nita tell you this. But you seem to have another wizard in the family."

"*What!*"

"Yes," Carl said, "that was my reaction too. Translation," he said to the computer.

"Translation of protected material requires double authorization by ranking Seniors and justification filed with Chief Senior for planet or plane," said the computer, sounding stubborn.

"What've you done to my machine!"

"The question," Tom said, getting up off the floor, "is more like, what has Dairine done to it? Sorry, Harry. This is a hell of a way for you to find out."

Nita watched her father take in a long breath. "Don't call her yet, Harry," said Tom. He laid a hand on the computer. "Confirmed authorization one zero zero three oblique zero two. We'll file the justification with Irina later. Translate."

The screen's contents abruptly turned into English. Nita's father bent over a bit to read it. " 'Oath accepted—' "

"This Oath," Carl said. "Type a-colon-heartcode."

The computer cleared its screen and displayed one small block of text in green. Nita was still while her father read the Wizards' Oath. There was movement behind her: she looked up and saw her mother, with a peppermill clutched forgotten in one hand, looking over her father's shoulder. Her face looked odd, and it wasn't entirely the green light from the computer screen.

"Dairine took that?" her father said at last.

"So did we, Daddy," Nita said.

"Yes, but—" He sat down on the edge of the desk, staring at the screen. "Dairine isn't quite like you two. . . ."

"Exactly. Harry, this is going to take a while. But first, you might call in Dairine. She did something careless this afternoon and I want to make sure she doesn't do it again."

Nita felt sorry for her father; he looked so pale. Her mother went to him. "What did she do?" she said.

"She went to Mars and left the door open," said Tom.

Nita's dad shut his eyes. "She went to Mars."

"Just like that. . . ." said her mother.

"Harry, Nita tells me she took you two to the Moon once, to prove a point. Imagine power like that . . . used irresponsibly. I need to make sure that's not going to happen, or I'll have to put a lock on some of her power. And there are other problems. The power may be very necessary for something. . . ." Carl looked stern but unhappy. "Where is she, Harry?"

"Dairine," Nita's dad said, raising his voice.

"Yo," came Dairine's voice from upstairs, her all-purpose reply.

"Come on down here a minute."

"Do I have to? I'm reading."

"Now."

The ceiling creaked a little, the sound of Dairine moving around her room. "What have I done to deserve this?" said Nita's father to the immediate universe.

"Harry," Carl said glancing at the computer

screen and away again, "this may come as a shock to you . . ."

"Carl, I'm beyond shocking. I've walked on the Moon without a spacesuit and seen my eldest daughter turn into a whale. That my youngest should go to Mars on a whim . . ."

"Well, as to what you've done to deserve it . . . you have a right to know the answer. The tendency for wizardry comes down to the kids through your side of the family."

That was a surprise to Nita, and as for her father, he looked stricken, and her mother looked at him with an expression that was faintly accusing. Carl said, "You're related to the first mayor of New York, aren't you?"

"Uh, yeah . . . he was—"

"—a wizard, and one of the best to grace this continent. One of the youngest Seniors in Earth's history, in fact. The talent in your line is considerable; too bad it missed you, but it does skip generations without warning. Was there something odd about one of your grandparents?"

"Why, my—" Nita's father swallowed and looked as if he was suddenly remembering something. "I saw my grandmother disappear once. I was about six. Later I always thought I'd imagined it. . . ." He swallowed again. "Well, that's the answer to why me. The next question is, why Dairine?"

"She's needed somewhere," said Carl. "The Powers value the status quo too highly to violate it

★ 72 ★

without need. It's what we're defending, after all. Somewhere out there is a life-or-death problem to which only Dairine is the answer."

"We just need to make sure she knows it," said Tom, "and knows to be careful. There are forces out there that aren't friendly to wizards—" He broke off suddenly as he glanced over at the computer screen. "Carl, you should see this."

They all looked at the screen. USER LOG, it said, and under the heading were listed a lot of numbers and what Nita vaguely recognized as program names. "Look at that," Tom said, pointing to one. "Those are the spells she did today, using the computer. Eighty-eight gigabytes of storage, all in one session, the latest one—at 16:52 hours. What utility uses that kind of memory?"

"That's what . . . about ten of five?" Nita's mother said. "She wasn't even *here* then. . . ."

The stairs creaked as Dairine came down them into the living room. She paused a moment, half-way, as well she might have done with all those eyes and all those expressions trained on her . . . her father's bewildered annoyance, her mother's indignant surprise, Tom's and Carl's cool assessment, and Nita's and Kit's expectant looks. Dairine hesitantly walked the rest of the way down.

"I came back," she said abruptly.

Nita waited for more. Dairine said nothing.

Nita's parents exchanged glances, evidently having the same thought: that a Dairine who said so little wasn't normal. "Baby . . ." her mother said, sounding uncertain, "you have some explaining to do."

But Carl stepped forward and said, "She may not be able to explain much of anything, Betty. Dairine's had a busy day with the computer. Isn't that so, Dairine?"

"I don't want to talk about it," Dairine said.

"I think it's more like you can't," said Carl.

"Look at the user log, Harry," Tom said from behind Nita and Kit. "Eighty-eight gigs spent on one program. A copy program. And run, as you say, when she wasn't even here. There's only one answer to that."

Slowly, as if he were looking at a work of art, Carl walked around Dairine. She watched him nervously. "Even with unlimited available memory and a computer running wizard's software," Carl said, "there's only so much fidelity a copy can achieve. Making hard copies of dumb machinery, even a computer itself, that's easy. Harry, look at the log: you'll see that this isn't the machine you bought. It's an exact copy of it. Dairine made it."

Carl kept walking around Dairine. She didn't move, didn't speak. "Carl, come on," Nita's father said from behind her, "cut it out. You're scaring her."

"I think not," Carl said. "There's only so much you can do with eighty gigs, as I said. Especially when the original is a living thing. The copy's re-

★ 74 ★

sponses are limited. See, there's something that lives inside the hardware, inside the meat and nervous tissue, that can't be copied. Brain can be copied. But mind—not so well. And soul—not at all. Those are strictly one to a customer, at least on this planet."

The air was singing with tension. Nita glanced at Kit, and Kit nodded, for he knew as well as she did the feel of a spell in the working. Carl was using no words or gestures to assist in the spell, nothing but the slow certain pressure of his mind as he thought in the Speech. "She copied the computer and took it to the city with her," Carl said, "and got away when she could. And when she left Earth, she decided—I'd imagine—that she wanted some time to sightsee. But, of course, you would object to that. So she copied something else, to buy herself some time."

The spell built and built in power, and the air sang the note ears sing in silence, but much louder. "Nothing not its own original can exist in this room," Carl said, "once I turn the spell loose. Harry, you're having trouble believing this, are you? You think I would treat your real daughter this way?"

Nita's father said nothing.

"Run," Carl said softly.

Dairine vanished. Air imploded into the place where she had been: manuals ruffled their pages in the sudden wind, papers flew up and slowly settled.

★ 75 ★

Behind them, the Apple simply went away; its monitor fell two inches to the desk with a loud thump, its screen gone dark, and the hard-drive cable slithered off the desk like a stunned snake and fell in coils to the floor.

Nita's father put his face in his hands.

Her mother looked sharply at Tom and Carl. "I've known you two too long to think you were toying with us," she said as Carl sat down slowly on the sofa, looking a bit pale. "You said something a moment ago about forces that weren't friendly . . ."

"Nita's told you some of what wizards are for," Tom said, looking at Carl in concern, then up again. "Balance. Maintenance of the status quo; protecting life. There are forces that are ambivalent toward life. One in particular . . . that held Itself aloof from creation, a long time ago, and when everyone else was done, created something none of the other forces had thought of: death. And the longest Death . . . the running-down of the Universe. The other Powers cast It out . . . and they've been dealing with the problem, and the Lone Power, ever since."

"Entropy," Nita's mother said, looking thoughtful. "That's an old story."

"It's the only story," Tom said. "Every sentient species has it, or learns it." He looked over at Nita's father, who was recovering somewhat. "I'm not about to pass judgment on whether the Lone One's invention was a good idea or not. There are cases for both sides, and the argument has been going on since time was set running. Every being that's ever lived has argued the case for one side or the other, whether it's been aware of it or not. But wizards fight the great Death, and the lesser ones, consciously . . . and the Entity that invented death takes our interference very personally. New wizards always meet it in one form or another, on their Ordeals. Some survive, if they're careful. Nita and Kit were careful . . . and they had each other's help."

" 'Careful' is not Dairine's style," Nita's mother said, sounding rueful. "And she's alone."

"Not for long," Tom said. "We'll track her, and see that she has help. But I think Nita will have to go. She knows Dairine's mind fairly well."

"I'm going too," said Kit.

Carl, still ashen from the exertion of his spell, shook his head. "Kit, your folks don't know you're a wizard. You might have to be gone for quite a while—and I can't sell you two a time warp as I did once before. My time-jurisdiction stops at atmosphere's edge."

"I'll tell them what I am," Kit said.

Nita turned and stared at him.

"I've been thinking about doing it for a while, since you told your folks," he said to her. "You handled it pretty well," he said to Nita's parents. "I should give my mom and dad the benefit of the doubt." The words were brave: but Nita noticed that Kit looked a little worried.

"Kit, you'll have to hurry," Tom said. "She's got a long lead on you, and the trail will get cold fast. Neets, where would Dairine want to go?"

Nita shook her head. "She reads a lot of science fiction."

Carl looked worried. "Has she been reading Heinlein?"

"Some," Nita said. "But she's mostly hot for Star Wars right now."

"That's something, at least. With luck she won't think of going much farther than a few galaxies over. Anything in particular about Star Wars?"

"Darth Vader," Kit said. "She wants to beat him up."

Tom groaned and ran one hand through his hair. "No matter what the reason," he said, "if she goes looking for darkness, she'll find it."

"But Darth Vader's not real!" said Nita's mother.

Tom glanced at her. "Not *here*. Be glad."

"A few galaxies over . . ." Nita's father said to no one in particular.

Carl looked grim. "We can track her, but the trail's getting cold; and at any rate Tom and I can't go with you."

"Now, wait a minute . . ." Nita's mother said.

Carl looked at her gently. "We're not allowed out of the Solar System," he said. "There are reasons.

For one thing, would you step out the door of a car you were driving?"

Nita's mother stared at him.

"Yes, well," Tom said. "We'll get you support. Wizards everywhere we can reach will be watching for you. And as for a guide—"

"I'll go," said Picchu abruptly, from the computer table.

Everyone stared, most particularly Nita's mother and father.

"Sorry, I should have mentioned," Carl said. "Peach is an associate. Bird, isn't this a touch out of your league?"

"I told you I was needed," Picchu said irritably. "And I am. I can see the worst of what's going to happen before it does; so I should be able to keep these two out of most kinds of trouble. But you'd better stop arguing and move. If Dairine keeps throwing away energy the way she's doing, she's going to attract Someone's attention . . . and the things It sends to fetch her will make Darth Vader look like a teddy bear by comparison."

Nita's mother looked at Carl and Tom. "Whatever you have to do," she said, "*do it!*"

"Just one question," Tom said to Picchu. "What do They need her for?"

"The Powers?" Picchu said. She shut her eyes.

"Well?"

"Reconfiguration," she said, and opened her eyes again, looking surly. "Well? What are you staring at? I can't tell you more than I know. Are we going?"

"Gone," Nita said. She headed out of the room for her manual.

"I'll meet you in the usual place when I'm done," Kit called after her, and vanished. Papers flew again, leaving Nita's mother and father looking anxiously at Carl and Tom.

"Powers," Nita heard her father say behind her. "Creation. Forces from before time. This is—this business is for saints, not children!"

"Even saints have to start somewhere," Carl said softly. "And it's always been the children who save the Universe from the previous generation, and remake the Universe in their own image."

"Just be glad yours are conscious of the fact that that's what they're doing," Tom said.

Neither of her parents said anything.

In her bedroom, Nita grabbed her manual, bit her lip, said three words, and vanished.

Randomization

Dairine did not go straight out of the Galaxy from Mars. Like many other wizards when they first cut planet-loose, she felt that she had to do a little local sightseeing first.

She was some while about it. Part of this was caused by discomfort. The jump from Earth to Mars, a mere forty-nine million miles, had been unsettling enough, with its feeling of first being pinned to a wildly rolling ball and then violently torn loose from it. But it hadn't been too bad. Piece o' cake, Dairine had thought, checking the transit directory in the computer. Somewhere out of the Solar System next. What's this star system? R Leporis? It's pretty close. . . . But she changed her mind, and headed for the moons of Jupiter instead

. . . and this turned out to be a good thing. From Mars to Jupiter, bypassing the asteroid belt, was a jump of three hundred forty-one million miles; and the huge differences between the two planets' masses, vectors, and velocities caused Dairine to become the first Terran to lose her lunch on Jupiter's outermost satellite, Ananke.

The view did more than anything else to revive her—the great banded mass of Jupiter swiftly traversing the cold night overhead, shedding yellow-red light all around on the methane snow. Dairine sat down in the dry, squeaky snow and breathed deeply, trying to control her leftover heaves. Where she sat, mist curled up and snowed immediately down again as the methane sublimated and almost instantly recrystallized to solid phase in the bitter cold. Dairine decided that getting used to this sort of travel gradually was a good idea.

She waited until she felt better, and then began programming—replenishing her air and planning her itinerary. She also sat for a while examining the transit programs themselves, to see if she had been doing something wrong to cause her to feel so awful . . . and to see if perhaps she could rewrite the programs a little to get rid of the problem. The programs were written in a form of MBASIC that had many commands which were new to her, but were otherwise mostly understandable. They were also complex: they had to be. Earth spins at seventeen thousand miles an hour, plows along its orbital path at a hundred seventy-five thousand, and the Sun takes it and the whole Solar System off toward the constellation Hercules at a hundred fifteen thousand miles an hour. Then the Sun's motion as one of innumerable stars in the Sagittarius Arm of the Galaxy sweeps it along at some two million miles an hour, and all the while relationships between individual stars, and those of stars to their planets, shift and change . . .

It all meant that any one person standing still on any planet was in fact traveling a crazed, corkscrewing path through space, at high speed: and the disorientation and sickness were apparently the cause of suddenly, and for the first time, going in a straight line, in a universe where space itself and everything in it is curved. Dairine looked and looked at the transit programs, which could (as she had just proved) leave you *standing* on the surface of a satellite three hundred fifty million miles away from where you started—not half embedded in it, not splatted into it in a bloody smear because of some forgotten vector that left you still moving a mile a second out of phase with the surface of the satellite, or at the right speed, but in the wrong direction. . . . Finally she decided not to tamper. A hacker learns not to fix what works . . . at least, not till it's safe to try. Maybe the transits'll get easier, she thought. At least now I know not to eat right before one. . . .

That brought up the question of food, which

needed to be handled. Dairine considered briefly, then used the software to open a storage pocket in otherspace. By means of the transit utility she then removed a loaf of bread, a bottle of mustard, and half a pound of bologna from the refrigerator back home, stuffing them into local otherspace where she could get at them. Mom 'n' Dad won't notice, she thought, and even if they do, what are they going to do about it? Spank my copy? Be interesting if they did. I wonder if I'd feel it. . . .

But there were a lot of more interesting things to consider today. Dairine stood up, got the computer ready, and headed out again, more cautiously this time. She stopped on Io, another one of Jupiter's moons, and spent a while (at a safe distance) watching the volcanoes spit white-hot molten sulfur ten miles out from the surface; sulfur that eventually came drifting back down, as a leisurely dusty golden snow, in the delicate gravity. Then she braced herself as best she could and jumped for Saturn's orbit, four hundred three million miles farther out, and handled it a little better, suffering nothing worse than a cold sweat and a few dry heaves, for the two planets were similar in mass and vectors.

Here there were twenty moons—too many for Dairine at the moment—but she did stop at Titan, the biggest satellite in the Solar System, and spent a while perched precariously on a peak slick with hydrogen snow, looking down thoughtfully at the methane oceans that washed the mountain's feet. Several times she thought she saw something move down there—something that was not one of the peculiar, long, high methane waves that the light gravity made possible. But the light was bad under the thick blue clouds, and it was hard to tell. She went on.

The jump to Uranus's orbit was a touch harder—six hundred sixty million miles to a world much smaller and lighter than the greater gas giants. Dairine had to sit down on a rock of Uranus's oddly grooved moon Miranda and have the heaves again. But she recovered more quickly than the last time, and sat there looking down on the planet's blurry green-banded surface for a long time. *Voyager 1* and *Voyager 2* had both been gravity-slung off toward alpha Centauri and were plunging toward the radiopause, the border of the Solar System, whistling bravely in the endless dark. Sitting here she could hear them both, far away, as she could hear a lot that the Sun's radio noise made impossible to hear closer in. That silent roar, too—the old ruinous echo of the Big Bang—was more audible here. How can I even hear it? she wondered briefly. But Dairine quickly decided it was just another useful side effect of the wizardry, and she got up and headed out as soon as she was better.

From Uranus to Neptune was one billion, one million miles. To her own surprise Dairine took it in stride, arriving standing up on Triton, one of Neptune's two largest moons, and with no desire to sit. Better! she thought, and looked around. There was very little to see: the planet was practically a twin of Uranus, except for its kinky partial rings, and the moons were barren. Dairine rubbed her arms. It was getting cold, even in the protective shell she had made for herself; her forcefields couldn't long stand this kind of chill. Out here the Sun was just one more star, bright, but not like a sun at all. The jump to Pluto was brief: she stood only for a minute or so in the barren dark and could hardly find the Sun at all, even by radio noise. Its roar was muted to a chilly whisper, and the wind on Pluto—it was summer, so there was enough atmosphere thawed to make a kind of wind—drank the heat away from her forcefields till in seconds she was shivering. She pulled the computer out. "Extrasystemic jump," she said hurriedly.

"Coordinates?"

"Read out flagged planets."

"Andorgha/beta Delphini, Ahaija/R Leporis, Gond/kappa Orionis, Irmrihad/Ross 614, Rirhath B/epsilon Indi—"

"The closest," said Dairine, feeling a touch nervous about this.

"Rirhath B. Eleven point four light-years."

"Atmosphere status?"

"Earthlike within acceptable parameters."

 ★ 86 ★

"Let's go," Dairine said.

"Syntax error 24," said the computer sweetly, "rephrase for accuracy."

"Run!"

A galaxy's worth of white fire pinned her to the rolling planet; then the forces she had unleashed tore Dairine loose and flung her out into darkness that did not break. For what seemed like ages, the old, old echoes of the Big Bang breaking over her like waves were all Dairine had to tell her she was still alive. The darkness grew intolerable. Eventually she became aware that she was trying to scream, but no sound came out, nothing but that roar, and the terrible laughter behind it.

—laughter?

—and light pierced her, and the universe roared at her, and she hit the planet with a feeling like dreaming of falling out of bed—

Then, silence. True silence this time. Dairine sat up slowly and carefully, taking a moment to move everything experimentally, making sure nothing was broken. She ached in every bone, and she was angry. She hated being laughed at under the best of circumstances, even when it was family doing it. Whatever had been laughing at her was definitely *not* family, and she wanted to get her hands on it and teach it a lesson. . . .

She looked around her and tried to make sense of things. It wasn't easy. She was sitting on a surface that was as slick white as glare ice in some places, and scratched dull in other spots, in irregularly shaped patches. Ranked all around her in racks forty or fifty feet high were huge irregular objects made of blue metal, each seeming made of smaller blocks stuck randomly together. The block things, and the odd racks that held them, were all lit garishly by a high, glowing green-white ceiling. *What is this, some kind of warehouse?* Dairine thought, getting to her feet.

Something screamed right behind her, an appalling electronic-mechanical roar that scared her into losing her balance. Dairine went sprawling, the computer under her. It was lucky she did, for the screaming something shot by right over her head, missing her by inches though she was flat on her face. The huge wind of its passing whipped her hair till it stung her face, and made her shiver all over. Dairine dared to lift her head a little, her heart pounding like mad, and stared after the thing that had almost killed her. It was another of the bizarre cube-piles, which came to a sudden stop in midair in front of one of the racks. A metal arm came out of the Tinkertoy works of the rack, snagged the cube-pile and dropped it clanging onto an empty shelf in the rack's guts.

Dairine pulled the computer out from under her and crawled carefully sideways out of the middle of the long white corridorlike open space, close to one of the metal racks. There she simply lay still for a moment, trying to get her wits back.

There was another scream. She held still, and saw another of the cubes shoot by a foot and a half above the white floor, stop and hover, and get snagged and shelved. Definitely a warehouse, she thought; and then part of the cube seemed to go away, popped open, and people came out.

They had to be people, she thought. Surely they didn't *look* at all like people; the four of them came in four different burnished-metal colors and didn't look like any earthly insect, bird or beast. Well, she said to herself, why should they? Nonetheless she found it hard to breathe as she looked at them, climbing down from their—vehicle?—was that their version of a car, and this a parking lot? The creatures—no, people, she reminded herself—the people were each different from all the others. They had bodies that came in four parts, or five, or six; they had limbs of every shape and kind, claws and tentacles and jointed legs. If they had heads, or needed them, she couldn't tell where they were. They didn't even look much like the same species. They walked away under the fluorescent sky, bleating at one another.

Dairine got up. She was still having trouble breathing. What've I been thinking of? She began to realize that all her ideas about meeting her first alien creatures had involved her being known, even expected. "Dairine's here finally," they were supposed to say, "now we can get something done"; and then she and they would set out to save the universe together. Because of her own blindness she'd gotten so excited that she'd jumped into a totally alien environment without orientation or preparation, and as a result she'd nearly been run over in a parking lot. My own fault, she thought, disgusted with herself. It won't happen again.

But in the meantime people were still getting out of that car: these people shorter and blockier than the first group, with more delicate legs and brighter colors. She picked up the computer, looked both ways most carefully up and down the "road," and went after them. "You still working?" she said to the computer.

"Syntax error 24—"

"Sorry I asked. Just keep translating."

As she came up behind the second group of people, Dairine's throat tightened. Everything she could think of to say to aliens suddenly sounded silly. Finally she wound up clearing her throat, which certainly needed it, as she walked behind them. Don't want to startle them, she thought.

They did absolutely nothing. Maybe they can't hear it. Or maybe I said something awful in their language! Oh, no— "Excuse me!" she said.

They kept walking along and said nothing.

"Uh, look," Dairine said, panting a little as she kept up with them—they were walking pretty fast—"I'm sorry to interrupt you, I'm a stranger here—"

The computer translated what Dairine said into a brief spasm of bleating, but the spidery people made no response. They came to the end of the line of racks and turned the corner. Ahead of them was what looked like a big building, made in the same way as the cars, an odd aggregate of cubes and other geometrical shapes stuck together with no apparent symmetry or plan. The scale of the thing was astonishing. Dairine suddenly realized that the glowing green-white ceiling was in fact the *sky*—the lower layer of a thick cloudy atmosphere, actually fluorescing under the light of a hidden, hyperactive sun—and her stomach did an unhappy flip as her sense of scale violently reoriented itself. I wanted strange, she thought, but not this strange!

"Look," she said to the person she was walking beside as they crossed another pathway toward the huge building, "I'm sorry if I said something to offend you, but please, I need some help getting my bearings—"

Dairine was so preoccupied that she bumped right into something on the other side of the street —and then yipped in terror. Towering over her was one of the first things to get out of the car, a creature seven feet high at least, and four feet wide, a great pile of glittering, waving metallic claws and tentacles, with an odd smell. Dairine backed away fast and started stammering apologies.

The tall creature bleated at her, a shocking sound up so close. "Excuse me," said the computer, translating the bleat into a dry and cultured voice like a BBC announcer's, "but why are you talking to our luggage?"

"Llp, I, uh," said Dairine, and shut her mouth. There they were, her first words to a member of another intelligent species. Blushing and furious, she finally managed to say, "I thought they were people."

"Why?" said the alien.

"Well, they were walking!"

"It'd be pretty poor luggage that didn't do that much, at least," said the alien, eyeing the baggage as it spidered by. "Good luggage levitates, and the new models pack and unpack themselves. You must have come here from a fair way out."

"Yeah," she said.

"My gate is about to become patent," the alien said. "Come along, I'll show you the way to the departures hall. Or are you meeting someone?"

They started to walk. Dairine began to relax a little: this was more like it. "No," she said, "I'm just traveling. But please, what planet is this?"

"Earth," said the alien.

Dairine was surprised for a second, and then remembered having read somewhere that almost every sentient species calls its own planet "Earth" or "the world" or something similar. "I mean, what do other people call it?"

"All kinds of things, as usual. Silly names, some of them. There'll be a master list in the terminal; you can check that."

"Thanks," Dairine said, and then was shocked and horrified to see a large triangular piece of the terminal fall off the main mass of the building. Except that it didn't fall more than a short distance, and then regained its height and soared away, a gracefully tumbling pyramid. "Does it do that often?" she said, when she could breathe again.

"Once every few beats," said the alien; "it's the physical-transport shuttle. Are you on holiday? Mind the slide, now."

"Yes," Dairine started to say, until the alien stepped onto a stationary piece of pavement in front of them, and instantly began slipping away from her toward the bizarre mass of the terminal building at high speed. The surprise was too sudden to react to: her foot hit the same piece of paving and slipped from under her as if she had stepped on ice. Dairine threw her arms out to break her fall, except that there wasn't one. She was proceeding straight forward, too, tilted somewhat backward, at about fifty miles an hour. Her heart hammered. It hammered worse when something touched her from behind; she whipped around, or tried to. It was only the alien's luggage, reaching out to tilt her forward so she stood straight. "What *is* this!" she said.

"Slidefield," the alien said, proceeding next to

her, without moving, at the same quick pace. "Inertia-abeyant selectively frictionless environment. Here we go. Which gating facility are you making for?"

"Uh—"

It was all happening too fast. The terminal building swept forward swift as a leaping beast, rearing up a thousand stories high, miles across, blotting out the sky. The slidefield poured itself at what looked like a blank silvery wall a hundred feet sheer. Dairine threw her arms up to protect herself, and succeeded only in bashing her face with the computer; the wall burst like a thin flat cloud against her face, harmless, and they were through.

"The Crossings," said the alien. "What do you think?"

She could not have told him in an hour's talking. The Crossings Hypergate Facility on Rirhath B is renowned among the Million Homeworlds for its elegant classical Lilene architecture and noble proportions; but Dairine's only cogent thought for several minutes was that she had never imagined being in an airline terminal the size of New Jersey. The ceiling—or ceilings, for there were thousands of them, layered, interpenetrating, solid and lacy, in steel and glass, in a hundred materials and a hundred colors—all towered up into a distance where clouds, real clouds, gathered; about a quarter-mile off to one side, it appeared to be raining. Through the high greenish air, under the softened light of the fluorescing sky that filtered in through the thousand roofs, small objects that might have been machines droned along, towing parcels and containers behind them. Beneath, scattered all about on the terminal floor, were stalls, platforms, counters, racks, built in shapes Dairine couldn't understand, and with long, tall signs placed beside them that Dairine couldn't begin to read. And among the stalls and kiosks, the whole vast white floor was full of people—clawed, furred, shelled or armored, upright or crawling, avian, insectile, mammalian, lizardlike, vegetable, mingling with forms that could not be described in any earthly terms. There were a very few hominids, none strictly human; and their voices were lost in the rustling, wailing, warbling, space-softened cacophony of the terminal floor. They hopped and stepped and leapt and walked and crawled and oozed and slid and tentacled and went in every imaginable way about their uncounted businesses, followed by friends and families and fellow travelers, by luggage floating or walking; all purposeful, certain, every one of them having somewhere to go, and going there.

Every one of them except Dairine, who was beginning to wish she had not come.

"There," said the alien, and Dairine was glad of that slight warning, because the slidefield simply stopped working and left her standing still. She waved her arms, overcompensating, and her stomach did a frightened wrench and tried once or twice, for old times' sake, to get rid of food that was now on Ananke.

"Here you are," said the alien, gesturing with its various tentacles. "Arrivals over there, departures over that way, stasis and preservation down there, !!!!! over there"—the computer made a staticky noise that suggested it was unable to translate something— "and of course waste disposal. You enjoy your trip, now; I have to catch up with my fathers. Have a nice death!"

"But—" Dairine said. Too late. The broad armored shape had taken a few steps into a small crowd, stepped on a spot on the floor that looked exactly like every other, and vanished.

Dairine stood quite still for a few minutes: she had no desire to hit one of those squares by accident. I'm a spud, she thought, a complete imbecile. Look at this. Stuck in an airport—something like an airport—no money, no ID that these people'll recognize, no way to explain how I got here or how I'm gonna get out—no way to understand half of what's going on, scared to death to move . . . and pretty soon some security guard or cop or something is going to see me standing here, and come over to find out what's wrong, and they're gonna haul me off somewhere and lock me up. . . .

The thought was enough to hurriedly start her walking again. She glanced around to try to make sense of things. There were lots of signs posted all over—or rather, in most cases, hanging nonchalantly in midair. But she could read none of them. While she was looking at one written in letters that at a distance seemed like Roman characters, something bumped into Dairine fairly hard, about shin-height. She staggered and caught herself, thinking she had tripped over someone's luggage. But there was nothing in her path at all. She paused, confused, and then tried experimentally to keep walking: the empty air resisted her. And then behind her someone said, "Your pardon," and slipped right past her: something that looked more or less like a holly tree, but it was walking on what might have been stumpy roots, and the berries were eyes, all of which looked at Dairine as the creature passed. She gulped. The creature paid her no mind, simply walked through the bit of air that had been resisting Dairine, and vanished as the thing with the tentacles had earlier. Just as it blinked out of existence, air whiffing past Dairine into the place where it had been, she thought she caught sight of what looked like a little triangular piece of shiny plastic or metal held in one of the thing's leaves.

A ticket, Dairine thought; and a little more wandering and watching showed her that this was the case. Wherever these little gates might lead, none of them would let you step on it unless you had the right ticket for it: probably the bit of plastic was a computer chip, programmed with the fact that you had paid your fare. So there was no need to fear

★ 97 ★

that she might suddenly fall unshielded into some environment where they were breathing methane or swimming around in lava.

Dairine began to wander again, feeling somewhat better. I can always sit down in a corner somewhere and program another jump, she thought. Be smart to do that now, though. In case something starts to happen and I want to get out quick. . . .

She looked for a place to sit. Off to one side was a big collection of racks and benches, where various creatures were hung up or lying on the floor. On a hunch she said to the computer, "Is it safe to sit over there?"

"Affirmative," said the computer.

Dairine ambled over in the direction of the racks and started searching for something decent to sit in.

The creatures she passed ignored her. Dairine found it difficult to return the compliment. One of the racks had what looked like a giant blue vampire bat hanging in it. Or no, it had no fur: the thing was actually more like a pterodactyl, and astonishingly pretty—the blue was iridescent, like a hummingbird's feathers. Dairine walked around it, fascinated, for quite a long time, pretending to look for a chair.

But there seemed to be no chairs in this particular area. The closest to a chairlike thing was a large low bowl that was full of what seemed to be purple

Jell-O . . . except that the Jell-O put up a long blunt limb of itself, the end of which swiveled to follow as Dairine passed. She hurried by; the effect was rather like being looked at by a submarine periscope, and the Jell-O thing had about as much expression. Probably wonders what the heck *I* am, she thought. Boy, is it mutual. . . .

Finally she settled for the floor. She brought up the utilities menu and started running down the list of planets again. . . . then stopped and asked for the "Help" utility.

"Nature of query," said the computer.

"Uh . . ." Dairine paused. Certainly this place was what she had thought she wanted—a big cosmopolitan area full of intelligent alien creatures. But at the same time there were hardly any hominids, and she felt bizarrely out of place. Which was all wrong. She wanted someplace where she would be able to make sense of things. But how to get that across to the computer? It seemed as though, even though it was magical, it still used and obeyed the laws of science, and was as literal and unhelpful as a regular computer could be if you weren't sufficiently familiar with it to know how to tell it what you wanted.

"I want to go somewhere else," she said to the machine.

"Define parameters," said the computer.

"Define syntax."

"Command syntax. Normal syntactical restrictions do not apply in the Help facility. Commands and appended arguments may be stated in collo-quial-vernacular form. Parameters may be subjected to Manual analysis and discussion if desired."

"Does that mean I can just talk to you?" Dairine said.

"Affirmative."

"And you'll give me advice?"

"Affirmative."

She let out a breath. "Okay," she said. "I want to go somewhere else."

"Acknowledged. Executing."

"No don't!" Dairine said, and several of the aliens around her reacted to the shriek. One of the holly tree people, standing nearby in something like a flowerpot, had several eyes fall off on the floor.

"Overridden," said the computer.

" 'Help' facility!" Dairine said, breathing hard. Her heart was pounding.

"Online."

"Why did you start doing that?!"

" 'OK' is a system command causing an exit from the 'Help' facility and a return to command level," said the computer.

"Do not run *any* program until I state the full command with arguments and end the sequence with 'Run'!"

"Affirmative," said the computer. "Syntax change confirmed."

Oh, Lord, Dairine thought, I've started messing with the syntax and I don't even *understand* it. I will never never use a program again till I've read the docs . . . "Good," she said. "The following is a string of parameters for a world I want to transit to. I will state 'end of list' when finished."

"Affirmative. Awaiting listing."

"Right. I want to go somewhere else."

"Transit agenda, confirmed. Specific arguments, please."

"Uhh . . ." She thought. "I want to go somewhere where there are going to be people like me."

"Noted. Next argument."

What exactly *was* I looking for? Darth Vader . . . She opened her mouth, then closed it again. I think I'll wait a bit on that one. "I want to go somewhere where I'm expected," she said.

"Noted. Next argument."

"Somewhere where I can use some of this magic."

"Argument already applies," said the computer. "You are using wizardry at this time."

Dairine made a face. "Somewhere where I can sit down and figure out what it means."

"Argument already applies. Documentation is available at this time."

Dairine sighed. "Somewhere where I will have *time* to sit down and figure out what it means."

"Incomplete argument. State time parameter."

"A couple of days. Forty-eight hours," she said then, before it could correct her syntax.

"Noted. Next argument."

"Somewhere—" One more time she stopped, considering the wild number of variables she was going to have to specify. And the truth was, she didn't know what she was after. Except . . . She looked around her conspiratorially, as if someone might overhear her. Indeed, she would have died if, say, Nita, should ever hear this. "Somewhere I can do something," she whispered. "Something big. Something that matters."

"Noted," said the computer. "Next argument."

"Uh . . ." The embarrassment of the admission out loud had driven everything out of her head. "End arguments," she said.

"Advisory," said the computer.

"So advise me."

"Stated number of arguments defines a very large sample of destinations. Stated number of arguments allows for interference in transit by other instrumentalities. Odds of interference approximately ninety-six percent."

That brought Dairine's chin up. "Let 'em try," she said. "The arguments stand."

"Instruction accepted. End advisory."

"Fine. List program."

"Transit program. Sort for Terran-type hominids along maximal space-time curvature. Sort for anticipated arrival, time continuum maximal but skewed to eliminate paradox. Sort for opportunity for intervention. Sort for data analysis period on close order, forty-eight hours. Sort for intervention curve skewed to maximal intervention and effect. End list."

"You got it," Dairine said. "Name listed program 'TRIP1.'"

"Named."

"Save it. Exit 'Help' facility."

"TRIP1 saved. Command level," said the computer.

"Run TRIP1."

"Running. Input required."

Dairine rolled her eyes at the mile-high ceiling. *Nita doesn't do it this way*, she thought. *I've watched her. She just reads stuff out of her book, or says it by heart. . . . Oh well, someone has to break new ground.* She stretched her legs out in front of her to keep them from cramping. "Specify," she said.

"Birth date."

"Twenty October nineteen seventy-eight," she said, looking out across the floor at the great crowd of pushing and jostling aliens.

"Place of birth."

"Three-eight-five East Eighty-sixth Street, New York City." The hospital had long since burned down, but Dairine knew the address: her dad had taken them all there to a German restaurant now on the site.

"Time of birth."

"Twelve fifty-five A.M."

"Favorite color."

"You have *got* to be kidding!" she said, looking at a particularly busy knot of aliens across the floor. Security guards, most likely: they were armed, in a big group, and looking closely at people.

"Favorite color."

"Blue." Or *were* these critters security guards? There had been other creatures walking around in the terminal wearing uniforms—as much or as little clothing of a particular shade of silvery green as each alien in question felt like wearing. And their weapons had been slim little blue-metal rods strapped to them. *These* creatures, though—they wore no uniforms, and their weapons were large and dark and looked nasty.

"Last book read," said the computer.

"Look," Dairine said, "what do you need to know this dumb stuff for?"

"Program cannot be accurately run without the enacting wizard's personal data. You have no data file saved at this time."

She made another face. Better not interfere, she thought, or you might wind up doing the breast-stroke in lava after all. "Oh, go on," she said.

"Last book read—"

"The Decline and Fall of the Roman Empire," said Dairine, looking with increasing unease at the armed bunch of aliens. They were not nice-looking

people. Well, *lots* of the people in here didn't look nice—that purple Jell-O thing for one—but none of them *felt* bad: just weird. But these creatures with the guns—they had an unfriendly look to them. Most of them were mud-colored warty-looking creatures like a cross between lizards and toads, but upright, and not nearly as pretty as a lizard or as helplessly homely as any toad. They went about with a lumpish hunchbacked swagger, and their eyes were dark slitted bulges or fat crimson blood-shot goggle-eyes. They looked stupid, and worse, they looked cruel. . . .

Oh, come on, Dairine told herself in disgust. Just because they're ugly doesn't mean they're bad. Maybe it's just some kind of military expedition, like soldiers coming through the airport on their way home for leave.

—but with their guns?

"Father's name," said the computer.

"Harold Edward Callahan," said Dairine. She was looking with a combination of interest and loathing at one of the warty creatures, which was working its way toward her. In one arm it was cradling a gun that looked big enough to shove a hero sandwich down. In its other hand, a knobby three-fingered one, it held the end of a leash, and strain-ing at the leash's far end was a something that looked more like the stuffed deinonychus at Natu-ral History than anything Dairine had ever seen. A skinny little dinosaur it was, built more or less along the lines of a Tyrannosaurus, but lithe and small and fleet. This one went all on its hind legs, its long thin tail stretched out behind it for balance: it went with a long-legged ostrichy gait that Dairine suspected could turn into an incredible sprint. The dinosaur on the warty alien's leash was dappled in startling shades of iridescent red and gold, and it had its face down to the floor as it pulled its master along, and the end of that long whiplike tail thrashed. And then it looked up from the floor, and looked right at Dairine, with eyes that were astonishingly innocent, and as blue as a Siamese cat's. It made a soft mewling noise that nonetheless pierced right through the noise of the terminal.

The warty thing looked right at Dairine too—and cried out in some language she couldn't understand, a bizarre soprano singing of notes like a synthesizer playing itself. Then it yanked the leash sharply and let the deinonychus go.

Dairine scrambled to her feet as the deinonychus loped toward her. Terrified as she was, she knew better than to try to run away from *this* thing. She slammed the computer's screen closed and waited. No kicks, she told herself, if one kick doesn't take this thing out, you'll never have time for a second —It leapt at her, but she was already swinging: Dairine hit the deinonychus right in the face with the computer and felt something crunch. Oh, please don't let it be the plastic, she thought, and then the impetus of the deinonychus carried it right into her, its broken jaw knocked against her face as it fell, she almost fell with it. Dairine stumbled back, found her footing, turned, and began to run.

Behind her more voices were lifted. Dairine ran like a mad thing, pushing through crowds wherever she could. *Who are they, why are they after me?* And where do I run . . .

She dodged through a particularly dense crowd and paused, looking for a corridor to run down, a place to hide. Nothing. This part of the Crossings was one huge floor, very few niches to take advantage of. But farther on, about half a mile away, it looked like the place narrowed. . . .

She ran. The noise behind her was deafening. There was some shooting: she heard the scream of blasterbolts, the sound that had set her blood racing in the movies. But now it wasn't so exciting. One bolt went wide over her head. It hit a low-floating bit of the ceiling off to one side of her, and she smelled the stink of scorched plastic and saw a glob of it fall molten to splat on the floor. Dairine sprinted past it, panting. She was a good runner, but she couldn't keep this up for much longer.

Bug-eyed monsters! her brain sang at her in terror. These weren't what I had in mind! "What *are* they—"

"Emissaries," said the computer, in a muffled voice since its screen was shut over its speaker.

Dairine kept running. "From where?"

"Indeterminate. Continue run?"

"If it'll get me out of here, *yes*—!"

"Last level of education finished—"

She told it, gasping, as she ran. She told it her mother's maiden name, and how much money her father made, and at what age she had started reading, and much more useless information. . . . And then while she was telling it what she thought of boys, something caught her by the arm.

It was a three-fingered hand, knobby, a slick dark green, and strong with a terrible soft strength that pulled her right out of her run and around its owner as if she were spinning around a pole. Dairine cried out at her first really close look at a bug-eyed monster. Its eyes were an awful milky red that should have meant it was blind, but they saw her too well entirely—and it sang something high at her and grabbed her up against it with its other hand, the nonchalant don't-hurt-it grasp of the upper arms that adults use on children, not knowing how they hate it . . . or not caring. Dairine abruptly recognized the BEM's song as laughter, once removed from the horrible low laughing she had seemed to hear in transit. And suddenly she *knew* what these things were, if not who. "*No!*" she screamed.

"Intervention subroutine?" said the computer, utterly calm.

Dairine struggled against the thing, couldn't get

leverage: all the self-defense she had been taught was for use on humans, and this thing's mass was differently distributed. Not too far away she heard more of the horrid fluting, BEMs with guns, coming fast. Half her face was rammed up against its horrible hide, and her nose was full of a stink like old damp coffee grounds. Her revulsion was choking her: the grasp of the thing on her was as unhuman as if she were being held by a giant cockroach . . . and Dairine *hated* bugs. *"Kill it!"* she screamed.

And something threw her back clear a good twenty feet and knocked her head against the floor . . .

Dairine scrambled up. The BEM was gone. Or rather, it wasn't a BEM anymore. It was many many little pieces of BEM, scattered among splatters of dark liquid all over the floor, and all over everything else in the area, including her. Everything smelled like an explosion in a coffeeshop.

Hooting noises began to fill the air. Oh, no, Dairine thought as she grabbed the computer up from the floor and began to run again. Now this place's own security people were going to start coming after her. They would ask her questions. And no matter how little a time they did that for, the BEMs would be waiting. If they waited. If they didn't just come and take her away from the port's security. And even if she killed every BEM in the place, more would come. She knew it.

She ran. People looked at her as she ran. Some of them were hominid, but not even they made any move to stop her or help her: they looked at her with the blank nervousness of innocent bystanders watching a bank robber flee the scene of the crime. Dairine ran on, desperate. It was like some nightmare of being mugged in a big city, where the streets are full of people and no one moves to help.

The blasterscreams were a little farther behind her. Maybe the one BEM's fate had convinced the others it would be safer to pick her off from a distance. But then why didn't they do that before?

Unless they wanted me alive . . .

She ran and ran. That laughter in the dark now pounded in her pulse, racing, and in the pain in the side that would shortly cripple her for running. Something she had read in Nita's manual reoccurred to her: Old Powers, not friendly to what lives: and one of the oldest and strongest, that invented death and was cast out . . . Part of her, playing cold and logical, rejected this, insisted she had no data, just a feeling. But the feeling screamed *Death!* and told logic to go stuff it somewhere. These things belonged to that old Power. She needed a safe place to think what to do. Home . . . But no. Take these things home with her? Her mom, her dad, these things would—

But maybe Nita and Kit could help—

But admit that she needed help?

Yes. No. *Yes—*

But without resetting the transit program, she couldn't even do that. No time . . .

"Can you run subroutines of that program before you finish plugging in the variables?" Dairine said, gasping as she ran.

"Affirmative."

"Then do it, as soon as you can!"

"Affirmative. Name of best friend—"

She wondered for a second whether 'Shash Jackson was still her best friend after she had cleaned him out of his record money three days ago. Then she gave his name anyway. Red lines of light lanced over her head as she ran. And here, the ceiling was getting lower, the sides of the building were closer, there were smaller rooms, places to go to ground. . . .

The stitch in her side was killing her. She plowed through a crowd of what looked like ambulatory giant squid on a group tour, was lost among them for a moment, in a sea of waving purple tentacles, tripping over their luggage, which crowded aside squawking and complaining—then came out the other side of them and plunged into a smaller corridor about the size of Grand Central Station.

She kept giving the computer inane information as she ran down the corridor, pushing herself to the far side of the stitch, so that she could reach someplace to be safe for a minute. There were more gates here, more signs and seating areas, and off to one side, a big shadowy cul-de-sac. She ran for it, any cover being better than none.

At the very end of her energy, she half ran, half stumbled in. It was unmistakably a bar. If she had had any breath to spare, she would have laughed with the dear familiarity of it, for it looked completely like other bars she had seen in airports when traveling with her folks and Nita—fairly dim, and crowded with tables and chairs and people and their bags. But no mere airport bar had ever had the kind of clientele that this place did. Tall furry things with too many arms, and squat many-legged things that looked to be wearing their organs on the outside, and one creature that seemed totally made of blinking eyes, all stared at Dairine over their snacks and drinks as she staggered in and past them, and not one of them moved.

Dairine didn't care. Her only thought was to hide. But she realized with horror that she could see no back way out of the place—only a dark red wall and a couple of what might have been abstract sculptures, unless they were aliens too. She heard the cries out in the terminal getting closer, and utter panic overcame her. Dairine shouldered and stumbled her way frantically among strange bodies and strange luggage in the semidarkness, hardly caring what she might or might not be touching. Impetus and blind terror crashed her right into a little table at the back of the room, almost upsetting both the table and the oddly shaped, half-full glass on it. And then something caught her and held her still.

After her experience out in the terminal, Dairine almost screamed at the touch. But then she realized that what held her were human hands. She could have sobbed for relief, but had no breath to spare. So rattled was she that though she stared right at the person who was steadying her, it took her precious seconds to see him. He was built slight and strong, wearing a white shirt and sweater and a long fawn-colored jacket: a fair-haired young man with quick bright eyes and an intelligent face. "Here now," he said, helping her straighten up, "careful!" And he said it in English!

Dairine opened her mouth to beg for help, but before she could say a word, those wise, sharp eyes had flickered over her and away, taking everything in.

"Who's after you?" the man said, quiet-voiced but urgent, glancing back at Dairine.

"I don't know what they are," she said, gasping, "but someone—someone bad sent them. I can lose them, but I need time to finish programming—"

Alarm and quick thought leapt behind those brown eyes. "Right. Here then, take these." The young man dug down in his jacket pocket, came up with a fistful of bizarrely shaped coins, and pressed them hurriedly into Dairine's free hand. "There's a contact transfer disk behind the bar. Step on it and you should materialize out in the service corridor. Follow that to the right and go out the first blue door you see, into the terminal. If I'm not mistaken, the pay toilets will be a few doors down on your left. Go in one of the nonhuman ones."

"The nonhuman—!" Dairine said, absolutely horrified.

"Quite so," the man said. "Right across the universe, that's one of the strongest taboos there is." And he grinned, his eyes bright with mischief. "No matter who's after you, it'll take them a bit to think of looking for you in there. And the locks will slow them down." He was on his feet. "Off you go now!" he said, and gave Dairine a fierce but friendly shove in the back.

She ran past a trundling robot barman, under the hinged part of the bartop and onto the transfer circle. On the other side of the bar, as Dairine began to vanish, she saw the fair man glance over at her to be sure she was getting away, and then pick up the iced tea he had been drinking. Glass in hand, he went staggering cheerfully off across the barroom in the most convincing drunk act Dairine could imagine, accidentally overturning tables, falling into the other patrons, and creating a mess and confusion that would slow even the BEMs up somewhat.

Dairine materialized in the service corridor, followed her instructions to the letter, and picked a rest room with a picture sign so weird, she couldn't imagine what the aliens would look like. She found out soon enough. She spent the next few minutes hastily answering the computer's questions while sitting on what looked like a chrome-plated lawn mower, while the tiled room outside her locked booth echoed with the bubbling screams of alien ladies (or gentlemen) disturbed in the middle of who knew what act.

Then the screams became quiet, and were exchanged for a horrible rustling noise, thick soft footfalls, and high fluting voices. The computer had asked Dairine whether she preferred Coke or Pepsi, and had then fallen silent for some seconds. "Are you done?" she hissed at it.

"Running. Data in evaluation."

"Get a move on!"

"Running. Data in evaluation."

The air filled with the scorch of burning plastic again. They were burning the lock of the booth.

"Can you do something to a few of them?" she whispered, her mouth going dry.

"Negative multitasking ability," said the computer.

Dairine put her head down on the computer, which was on her knees, and took what she suspected might be her last breath.

The lock of the booth melted loose and the door fell in molten globs to the floor. Dairine sat up straight, determined to look dirty at the BEMs, if she could do nothing else.

The door swung open.

And "Multiple transit," said the computer, "executing now," and the jump-sickness grabbed Dairine and twisted her outside in. Perhaps not understanding, the BEMs fluted in rage and triumph and reached into the booth. But Dairine's insides went cold as dimly she felt one of them swing a huge soft hand through where her middle was: or rather, where it no longer was completely—the transit had begun. A second later, heat not wholly felt stitched through her arms and legs as shots meant to cripple her tore through where they almost were, and fried the back of the stall like an egg. Then starlight and the ancient black silence pierced through her brain; the spell tore Dairine free of the planet and flung her off Rirhath B into the long night.

She never found out anything about the man who helped her. Nor did he ever find out anything more about her. Pausing by the door of the pay toilet, after being released from station security some hours later, and being telepathically sensitive (as so many hominids are), he could sense only that some considerable power had been successfully exercised there. Satisfied with that, he smiled to himself and went on about his travels, just one more of the billions of hominids moving about the worlds. But many millions of light-years later, in some baking wilderness under a barren, brilliant sky, a bitterly weary Dairine sat down on a stone and cried for a while in shock at the utter strangeness of the universe, where unexpected evil lives side by side with unexpected kindness, and neither ever seems quite overcome by the other. . . .

Variables

It took Nita a few minutes to pull her supplies together and get ready for the trip. Every wizard has favorite spells, so familiar and well used that diagrams and physical ingredients like eye of newt aren't needed for them. But most spells, and particularly the most powerful ones, need help in bending space—some specific kind of matter placed in specific relationship to the wizard and the words being used and the diagram or formula asserting the wizard's intent. Some of the kinds of matter used for these purposes can be odder even than eye of newt (which used to be used for teleportation spells until polyethylene was invented). And this being the case, most wizards have a cache, a place where they keep the exotica necessary in their work.

Nita's cache was buried in a vacant lot next door to her house, all carefully wrapped in a plastic garbage bag. Being a wizard, she had no need to dig the bag up: a variant of the spell Kit had used on the bricks let her feel around under the ground for the moment it took her to find what she wanted. The objects didn't look like much—half a (seemingly) broken printed-circuit board; a plastic packet containing about two teaspoonsful of dirt; and a gimbal from a 1956 Philco Pilot television set.

That last piece she juggled appreciatively from hand to hand for a moment. It was certainly unlikely looking, a busted bit of junk that any normal person would trash without a second thought. But the configuration into which the space-time continuum bent itself around this gimbal was unique, and invested with a power that the informed wizard could exploit. *Everything* bent spacetime, of course: anything consisting of either matter or energy had no choice. But some things bent it in ways that produced specific physical effects. . . . and no one, not even the wizards specializing in theoretical research, had any idea yet as to *why*. The atoms and mass and inherent spatiotemporal configuration of, say, water, bent existence around them to produce an effect of wetness. The electrons and plasma and matter and gravity of a star produced effects of heat and light. And a busted-off piece of gimbal from an ancient TV set . . .

Nita smiled a bit, put the gimbal carefully in her pocket, and said three more words.

Her room was dark. She flipped the light on and went digging in the mess off to one side for her knapsack. Into it she stuffed her manual, the gimbal and packet and circuit board.

"Nita?"

"Uh-huh," she said.

The stairs creaked. Then her mother was standing in the doorway, looking upset.

"You said you were going to clean your room today," her mother said in a tired voice.

Nita looked up . . . then went hurriedly to her mother and grabbed her and hugged her hard. "Oh, thanks," she said, "thanks, *thanks* for saying something normal!"

Her mother laughed, a sound that had no happiness about it at all, and hugged her back. After a moment her mother said, "She won't be normal when she gets back, will she?"

Nita took a moment to answer. "She won't be like she was, not completely. She can't. She's on Ordeal, Mums: it changes you. That's what it's about." Nita tried to smile, but it felt broken. "She might be better."

"Better? Dairine?" her mother said, sounding a touch dry. Nita's smile began to feel less broken, for that sounded more like her mother.

"Oh, c'mon, Mom, she's not that bad—" Then Nita stopped herself. What am I saying! "Look, Mom," she said, "she's real smart. Sometimes that makes me want to stuff her in the toilet, but it's going to come in handy for her now. She's not stupid, and if the wizards' software in the computer is anything like our manuals, she'll have some help if she can keep her head and figure out what to ask for. If we get a move on, we'll catch up with her pretty quick."

"If you can find her."

Nita's father loomed up in the doorway in the darkness, a big silver-haired shadow.

Nita swallowed. "Daddy, she'll leave a trail. Using wizardry changes the shape of the space-time continuum . . . it's like cutting through a room full of smoke with a knife. You can see where the knife's been. Knowing Dairine, she won't be making any effort to cover her trail . . . at least not just yet. We can follow her. If she's in trouble, we'll get her out of it. But I can't stay to talk about it. Kit needs me quick, and I can't do a lot for Dari without him. Some . . . but not as much. We work best as a team."

Her mother gave her father a look that Nita could make nothing of. "When do you think you three will be back?" said her father.

"I don't know," Nita said. She thought to say something, stopped herself, then realized that they had a right to know. "Mums, Dad, look. We might not be able to bring her back right away. It's *her* Ordeal. Until she solves the problem she's supposed to be the answer to, if we pull her back, awful things could happen. If we'd copped out of ours, this whole world would be different. And believe me, you wouldn't have liked the difference." She swallowed at the thought of something like that leaning, threatening darkness waiting for Dairine to confront it . . . something like that, but *much* worse.

They stood and looked at her.

"I've gotta go," she said, and slung her knapsack on, and hugged them hard, first her dad and then her mom again. Her father took a long time to let her go. Her mother's eyes were still troubled, and there was nothing Nita could do about it, nothing at all.

"I'll clean up in here as soon as I get home," Nita said, "I promise."

The trouble didn't go out of her mother's face, but half her mouth made a smile.

Nita said three words, and was gone.

Our home Galaxy is a hundred thousand light-years across, five thousand light-years thick at the core. The billion stars that make it up are scattered through some four quadrillion cubic miles of space. It is so vast that a thought can take as long as two seconds to cross it.

But Dairine was finding the entirety of the Milky

★ 123 ★

Way much too small to get lost in. She got out of it as soon as she could.

The program the computer was still writing to take her to safety was a multiple-jump program, and that suited her fine: her pursuers seemed to have trouble following her. But not enough trouble. She came out, after that first jump from Rirhath B, on some cold world whose sky she never saw: only a ceiling of gray. She was standing in a bleak place, full of what at first sight looked like old twisted, wind-warped trees, barren of any leaves, all leaning into a screaming wind that smelled of salt water. Dairine clutched the computer to her and stared around her, still gasping from her terror in a rest room twelve trillion miles away.

With a slow creaking sound, one of the trees pulled several of its roots out of the ground and began to walk toward her.

"No way!" Dairine shrieked. "Run another subroutine!"

"Running," said the computer, but it took its sweet time about it—and just as the world blinked out and the spell tore her loose from the hillside, Dairine felt wind on her skin—a wind that smelled of coffee grounds. The BEMs had popped right in behind her.

She popped out again, this time in the middle of a plain covered with sky-blue grass under a grass-green sky. She shook the computer in frustration.

★ 124 ★

"Program running," the computer insisted.

"Sure, but they're following us! How are they doing it? Are we leaving a trail somehow?"

"Affirmative," said the computer calmly, as if Dairine should have known this all along.

"Well, *do* something about it!"

"Advisory," said the computer. "Stealth procedures will decrease running speed. Stealth procedures are not one hundred percent effective due to inherent core-level stability of string functions—"

"I'll settle! And if we don't have to keep wasting time running subroutines," Dairine said, exasperated, "you'll have more time to run the main program, won't you!"

"Affirmative. Execute stealth?"

"Before someone executes *me*, yeah!"

Once again the spell took hold of Dairine and ripped her free of gravity and light. At least, she thought, this time the BEMs hadn't appeared before she vanished herself. Maybe we can gain a little ground. We'd better. . . .

Another reality flicked into being around her. She was in the middle of a city: she got a brief impression of glassy towers that looked more grown than built, and people rushing around her and avoiding her in the typical dance of city dwellers. This might almost have been New York, except that New Yorkers had only a small percentage of the legs these people had. "Don't stop," she said. "How much range have you got?"

"Infinite," said the computer, quite calmly.

"While still running the main program?"

"Affirmative."

She thought for a second. "The edge of the Local Group might be far enough. Go."

The spell seized her out of the crowd and flung her into the dark again. Over and over Dairine jumped, becoming less and less willing to stop, until finally strange vistas were flickering past her with the speed of some unutterably strange slide show being run in fast-forward by a bored lecturer. She passed right through the coronation parade of one of the Anarchs of Deleian IV and never noticed it: she stood for only a second on a chilly little planetoid being fought over by two desperate interstellar empires (and also missed the nova bomb that turned the planetoid into plasma several minutes later); she stood on the metallic upper floors of a planet that was one great library full of three galaxies' knowledge, and she never knew what it was, and probably at that point would not have cared. Only once Dairine paused for more than a few seconds, on a red sandstone promontory with a pinkish sea crashing at its foot, and no signs of life anywhere under the bloated red sun that dyed the water. "Are they still following?" she said.

"Probability high, but at a greatly increased distance."

"You have enough time to finish the main program?"

"Affirmative."

"Do it, then."

She sat down on a rock and looked out at the water, while the computer's disk drive chirred softly to itself. The fat red sun slipped horizonward as she watched, and Dairine looked at it and noticed through the sunset haze that it had a companion, a little blue-white dwarf star that was slowly sucking the red giant's matter out of it in an accretion spiral of tarnished gold. She shook her head. Once she would have given anything to sit here and watch this. Now, though, the hair was rising on the back of her neck, and her back prickled, and all she wanted in the world—the worlds—was to get out of here and end up where she could hide.

She shivered. I never want to smell coffee again, she thought. They had unquestionably been sent after her by what had laughed at her in the dark. The Lone Power, the manual utility had called It. Well, at least she didn't hear It laughing anymore while she was in transit. Then again, that might not be good. I'm running pretty fair rings around Its people. It's probably real annoyed at me.

And then she tossed her head and grinned, her nasty grin. Let It be, then. I'm not going to be running for long. I'm going to turn around and give It something to think about.

If I can just figure out what to do, and find a weapon. . . .

"Done," said the computer.

"Is this going to be a bad jump?" Dairine said.

"Transit may have significant physiological effects," said the computer.

"Okay," Dairine said. "Go for it." And she clenched her jaw.

The computer was understating. The jump was a hundred times worse than the first long one, an eternity of being torn, squeezed out of shape, pulled, hammered on, sliced by lines of force thinner than any hair and sharp as swords. Dairine hung on, unable even to scream. The transit broke for an instant on the surface of some planet as the program finished one jump subroutine, in a frozen flash of light and time too sudden to let any of the scream out, then pushed Dairine outside the universe and crushed her under its weight again. Then flash, and again; flash, and again: flash, flash, flash, flash, through a voiceless darkness a trillion years heavy and empty as entropy's end. This was the worst after all, the aloneness, total, no one to hear the scream she could not utter, not even the One who laughed—flash, flash, flash—

—and then the crushing ceased, and the spell flung Dairine down on something flat and hard and chill, and she flopped down like a puppet with its strings cut and just lay there as she had not done since Ananke. Her stomach flipped, but this was becoming so commonplace that Dairine was able to ignore it and just lie there and pant for a few seconds.

Silence. Not that awful emptiness, but a more normal one: probably just lack of air. Dairine levered herself up painfully on her elbows and looked at the surface under her hands. It was dimly lit, and smooth as the garage floor on Rirhath B had been. Smoother, in fact. It was hard to tell colors in this dimness, but the surface wasn't plain white. Dapples of various shades seemed to overlap and shade one another in the depths of it, as delicately as if they had been airbrushed: and there was a peculiar translucence to the surface, as if it were glass of some kind.

Cautiously, Dairine got up to a kneeling position and straightened to look around. Now *this* is weird, she thought, for the surface on which she knelt, stretched on so far into the distance that she scrubbed at her eyes briefly, not quite believing them. The horizon seemed much farther away than it could ever be on Earth. Must be a much bigger planet, she thought. But the thought did not make that immense vista any easier to grasp. It seemed to curve *up* after a while, though she was sure it was perfectly flat: the illusion was disturbing. Over the horizon hung starry space, the stars close and bright. Off to the sides the view was the same: here and there conical outcroppings of rock might break the pure and perfect flatness of it all, looking as if Picasso had dropped them there . . . but otherwise there was nothing but that endless, pale, slick-smooth surface, dappled with touches of dim subtle color, in huge patches or small ones.

Dairine stood up and turned around to look for the computer. It was behind her, at her feet: she bent to pick it up—

—and forgot about doing so. Before her, past the razory edge of that impossibly distant horizon, the galaxy was rising.

It was not her own. The Milky Way is a type S0 spiral, a pinwheel of stars. This was a barred spiral, type SB0, seen almost face-on: an oval central core, two bars jutting from its core, one from each end of the starry oval, and each bar having a long curved banner or stream of stars curling away from it. Dairine had seen a hundred pictures of them and had mostly been fascinated by that central bar, wondering what gravitational forces were keeping it in place. But now she was seeing such a galaxy as few, even wizards, ever see one—not as a flat, pale far-off picture but as a three-dimensional object near at hand, rich with treasuries of stars in a spectrum's worth of colors, veiled about with diamonded dust on fire with ions and glowing, dominating a third of even that immense horizon, seeming frozen though in the midst of irresistible motion, its starry banners streaming back in still and complex glory from the eye-defeating blaze of the core. Dairine slowly folded back down to the kneeling position and just watched it, watched it rise.

She weighed just a little less than she would have on Earth; but the spiral rose quickly, for a planet of this size. Must not be a very dense planet, Dairine thought. All light elements—though most of her paid no attention to the analysis, being busy with more important matters . . . this light, the terror and the wonder of it. *This,* was what she had come for. The computer had hit it right on. This planet's sun must be in one of the galaxy's satellite globular clusters. . . . As such distances went, she was close to that spiral: no more than ten or twenty thousand light-years above its core. But the thought of distances broke her mood. She pulled the computer close. "Did we lose them?" she said to it.

"Pursuit has halted forty trillion light-years from this location and is holding there."

"Forty *trillion* . . ." That was beyond the reach of the farthest telescopes, over the event horizon generated by the Big Bang itself: galaxies past that point were traveling with intrinsic velocities faster than light, and so could not be seen. It was questionable whether such bodies could even really be considered in the same universe as Earth.

"Long way from home," she said softly. "Okay. I have at least a couple days to rest and do some research, huh?"

"Affirmative."

She sat back on her heels and watched the light rise until the last delicate streamers of light from the barred spiral arms were all the way above the horizon. "I want all the details about this star system," she said. "Planets, what kind of star, who lives here if anybody, who's been here before. Get to work."

"Working," said the computer, and its screen went to the usual menu configuration while it sat silently, getting the information for her.

"Can you multitask now?" Dairine said.

"Affirmative."

"Good."

She selected the "Manual" function and began sorting through it for background material on the Lone One. There has to be something I can use against It, she thought, a weapon of some kind, a weakness. . . . She instructed the manual's research facility to sort for past conflicts of wizards with the Lone Power or its representatives, and was shocked and horrified to find the equivalent of twenty or thirty thousand pages' worth of abstracts. She skimmed ten or fifteen of them in reverse order, on a hunch, and was momentarily surprised to find an abstract of Nita's last active mission. Fascinated, Dairine began to read . . . and became horrified again. There had been some kind of ceremony in the waters off Long Island, a sort of underwater passion play with whales as the celebrants—and Nita, to save the East Coast and make this ceremony work, had volunteered to be eaten by a shark! Nita? My sister? Do anything braver than cross the street? The idea was ridiculous . . . but Dairine knew that this computer had better things to do than lie to her. She read the rest of the abstract with her insides turning cold. Nita had knowingly taken on that Lone Power face-to-face and had managed to come out of it alive. Whereas Dairine had been glad enough to run away and lose things that couldn't be more than Its lesser henchmen . . .

Dairine pushed that thought away resolutely. She was helped by her stomach, which growled at her.

When *did* I last eat? she wondered. She told the computer to sort through and save the descriptions of encounters with the Power that had been successful, and then got out of the "Manual" into the "Hide" facility. A moment's poking around among the options, and she had retrieved her loaf of bread, bologna, and mustard. Dairine sat there in cheerful anticipation for a few seconds, undoing the bread and bologna, and it wasn't until she got the mustard jar lid unscrewed that she realized she had no knife. "Oh, well," she said, and went back into the "Hide" facility to snitch one from the silverware drawer at home. But "Illegal function call," said the computer: a little sullenly, she thought.

"Explain."

"Out of range for transit function from stated location."

Dairine made a face. She had no idea of the coordinates of any closer silverware drawer. "Cancel," she said, and made do with her fingers.

Some minutes later she had a sandwich and a half inside her, and was thinking (as she finished getting herself more or less clean) that it was a good thing she liked mustard. Dairine brushed the crumbs off onto the slick surface she sat on and looked at it, mildly curious. It wasn't freezing cold to sit on, like the stones of Mars or Pluto: yet her shields were still snowing water vapor gently into the vacuum around her whenever she moved, telling her that the above-surface temperature was the usual cold of deep space. Geothermal? she wondered. Maybe some volcanic activity—that would explain those funny conical shapes against the horizon. . . . She thumped the computer in a friendly fashion. "You done yet?" she said.

"Specify."

Dairine rolled her eyes. But there was no escaping the GIGO principle—"garbage in, garbage out," as the programmers said. Give the poor machine incomplete questions or instructions and you would get incomplete answers back. This thing might be magic, but it was still a computer. "Are you done with the survey of this area?"

"Still running."

"How much longer?"

"Three point two minutes."

Dairine sat back to wait, absently rubbing the surface she sat on. The smoothness of it was strange: not even the maria on the Moon were this smooth. Volcanic eruption, maybe. But not the way it usually happens, with the lava flowing down the volcano's sides and running along the surface. Not enough gravity for it to do that, I guess. Maybe it's like the volcanoes on Io: the stuff goes up high in tiny bits or droplets, then comes down slowly in the low gravity and spreads itself out very smooth and even. It must go on all the time . . . or else there can't be much in this system in the way of even tiny meteors. Maybe both. She shook her head. It spoke of an extremely ancient planet—which made sense this far out in space. . . .

"Ready," the computer said, and Dairine hunkered over it to listen. "Local system stats. System age: close order of eight billion years. One primary, type S6 star, off main sequence, time from fusion ignition: close order of five billion years. One associated micro-black hole in variable orbit. One planet, distance from primary: six hundred twelve million miles. Planet diameter: fifty-six thousand miles. Planet circumference: one hundred seventy-five thousand miles—" And Dairine gulped, understanding now why that horizon ran so high. The planet was almost seven times the size of Earth. "Atmosphere: monatomic hydrogen, less than one fifty-millionth psi Terran sea level. Planetary composition: eighty percent silicon in pure form and compounds, ten percent iron and mid-sequence metals, seven percent heavy metals, one percent boron, one percent oxygen, one percent trace elements including frozen gases and solid-sequence halogens. Power advisory—"

The screen, which had been echoing all this, went blank. Dairine's stomach flip-flopped, from fear this time. "What's the matter?"

"System power levels nearing critical. Range to alternative-power claudication exceeded. Outside power source required."

Dairine paused, feeling under her hand that oddly non-cold surface. "Can you use geothermal?" she said.

"Affirmative."

"Is there some way you can tap what's in this planet, then?"

"Affirmative," said the computer. "Authorization for link."

"Granted," Dairine said, mildly surprised: she couldn't remember the computer ever asking her for permission to do anything before. Maybe it was a safety feature. Then she began to sweat a little. Maybe such a safety feature was wise. If the computer fried its chips somehow and left her without life support, sitting here naked to vacuum at heaven knew how many degrees below zero . . .

She watched the screen nervously as scrambled characters flashed on it, and for several awful seconds the screen blanked. Then the menu screen reasserted itself, and Dairine breathed out, slowly, while the computer went back to running the program it had been working on. "Link established," said the computer in absolute calm. "Planetary history—"

"Just print it to the screen, I'll read it," Dairine said, and started to pick the computer up: then paused. "Is it all right to move you? Will that hurt the link?"

"Negative effect on link."

She lifted the computer into her lap and went on reading. It was as she had thought. The planet periodically became volcanically active, and the volcanoes spewed a fine mist of lava all over the landscape, airbrushing the glassy surface on a gigantic scale with vividly colored trace elements. Subsequent layering muted the colors, producing the dappled translucence she sat on. Dairine hit the carriage return for another screenful of data, and the screenful appeared—and her stomach flipped again.

This unique structure becomes more interesting when considering the physical nature of the layering. Some 92% of the layers consi1t of chemically pure sil1co1,1 pred1spo11ng th1 ag1111ate to ele1111111ducti111111111111111111111111111
1111111111111111111111111111111111111111111111111111
1111111111111111111111111111111111111111111111111111
1111111111111111111111111111111111111111111111111111
1111111111111111111111111111111111111111111111111111
1111111111111111111111111111111111111111111111111111
1111111111111111111111111111111111111111111111111111
1111111111111111111111111111111111111111111111111111
1111111111111111111111111111111111111111111111111111
1111111111111111111111111111111111111111111111111111
1111111111111111111111111111111111111111111111111111

"I blew it up," Dairine whispered, horrified. "Oh, no, oh, no, I fried its brains. I blew it up." She took a deep breath, not sure how many more of them she was going to get, and gingerly hit the carriage return to see what would happen. . . .

Pattern Recognition

Nita popped out into a canopy of starlit darkness and a carpet of dim light, breathing very hard. Earth's gravity well was no joke: pushing her own mass and enough air to breathe for a while up out of that heavy pull was a problem. She walked over to a boulder, dusted it off, and sat down, panting, to admire the view while she waited for Kit.

The "usual place" where they met was, of course, the Moon. Nita liked it there; working, and thinking, were always easy there, in the great silence that no voices but astronauts' and wizards' had broken since the Moon's dust was made. This particular spot, high in the lunar Caucasus mountain chain, was a favorite of Kit's—a flat-topped peak in a wild, dangerous country of jagged gray-white alps, cratered and pocked by millennia of meteoric bombardment. Piles of rocktumble lay here and there, choking the steep valleys where the sheer heat and cold of the lunar days had been enough to flake solid rock away from itself in great glassy or pumicey chunks. Off to one side, the pallid rim of the little crater Calippus scraped razor-sharp against the sky, and over it hung the Earth.

The Moon was at first quarter, so the Earth was at third, a blinding half-world: blazing blue-green, almost painful to look at until the eyes got used to it. It shed a cool faint blue-white light over everything. A curl of white stormweather lay over the northwestern Pacific, and there vanished; for down the middle of it the terminator ran, the edge of night, creeping ever so slowly toward the west. Most of North America lay in the darkness, and city lights lay golden in faint glittering splashes and spatters with brighter sparkling patches under the Great Lakes and on the California coast.

Nita shrugged out of her knapsack, opened it and rechecked the contents. It was a good assortment: varied enough to handle several different classes of spell, specific enough to those classes to let her save some power for herself.

She pulled her manual out and started paging through it for the "tracker" spell that she and Kit would need when he got here. It was actually a variant of the one he had threatened to put on Dairine in the city: this one hunted for the characteristic charged "string residue" left in space by the passage of a wizard's transit spell through it. Nita's specialty was astronomy, so she had been shocked to find that "empty" space wasn't actually empty, and even the hardest vacuum had in it what physicists called "strings," lines of potential force that have nothing to do with any of the forces physicists understand. Wizards, of course, could use them: much of what passes for telekinesis turns out in fact to be string manipulation. The tracker spell made most elegant use of it. And once we find her, Nita thought, I'm gonna tie a few of those strings around her neck. . . .

But it didn't do to start a wizardry in such a mood. Nita pulled her space pen out of her pocket, kicked some of the larger rocks out of her way— they bounced off down the mountain as slowly as soap bubbles—and began drawing the circle for the transit spell.

It was becoming an old familiar diagram, this one. The basic circle, knotted with the wizard's knot: her own personal data, reduced by now (after much practice) to one long scrawl in the precise and elegant shorthand version of the Speech: Kit's data, another scrawl, over which she took even more care than her own. What a wizard names in the Speech, is defined so: inaccurate naming can alter the nature of the named, and Nita liked Kit just the way he was. A third long scrawl of shorthand for Picchu: Nita looked oddly at some of the variables in it, but Tom had given her the data, and he certainly knew what he was doing. Then the internal diagrams, the "intent" factors. The point of origin, the intended point of arrival or vector of travel; the desired result; the time parameters and conditional statements for life-support; the balloon-diagram for the ethical argument . . .

Nita wiped sweat and grit off her face, and muttered at the incessant hissing in the background. Dust flew freely in one-sixth gravity, and got in everything: after you went to the Moon, you took a shower, for the same reasons you take one after a haircut. But there wasn't much more to do here. She finished the last few strokes of the notations in the environmental-impact statement and stood up, rubbing her back and checking her work for spelling errors.

It was all in order. But that hissing. . . .

She sat down again, feeling nervous. Facility with the Speech, as with any other language, increases with time. After several months of working in a sort of pidgin Speech, Nita was finally beginning to think in it, and the results were sometimes upsetting. Once upon a time, it had been quiet on the Moon when she visited. But no more. Her more accustomed mind heard a sound in the darkness now: a low low sound like a breath being let out, and out, and out forever. The astronomer part of her knew what it was—the so-called four-degree radiation that was all that was left of the universe's birth. Normally only radio telescopes set to the right frequency could hear it. But Nita wasn't normal. Nor was the sound just a sound to her. In it she could hear the sound of consciousness, life, as plainly as she had used to be able to hear Kit think. *That* sensitivity had decreased over time; but this one was increasing, it seemed in the deep silence, by the minute. It upset her. Suddenly the universe, that had seemed so empty, now felt crammed full of powers and intelligences that might not need planets, or bodies. And Dairine was out there in the middle of them, mucking around in her inimitable fashion. . . . Nita found herself wishing that Kit would hurry up. She very much wanted to see that cheerful face, to hear at least his voice, if not his sassy, loud cast of thought, always with that slight Hispanic accent to it. . . .

Long time since we heard each other think. . . .

She had been wondering about that. Idly she began flipping through the manual, turning pages. Maybe the index— But the index did her no good: she couldn't think what heading to look under. "Come on," she muttered to the book, "give me a hand here, I don't have all day."

It was that hissing that was making her ill-tempered, she realized. A thought occurred to her, and she was glad she hadn't completely cleaned out her knapsack the other day. She reached into it and pulled out a tangle of cord, and a pair of earphones, and her Walkman. It was a Christmas present from her mother—the best of any present Nita had gotten last year, for she loved music and liked walking through her day with a soundtrack. Now she riffled through the pages of her manual, squinting at them in the pale Earthlight, while rock sang softly in the earphones.

Diagrams . . . She skipped that whole section, not without another glance over at Kit's name scrawled in the motionless, powdery lunar dust. He was all there: at least, he seemed to think so—it was mostly the description of himself he had carefully worked out. Of course, after their first few spells Nita had looked over his shoulder and suggested a couple additions to the data—his fondness for chocolate ice cream (which he had instantly admitted), and his craziness for poetry, especially Shakespeare (which embarrassed him, and which he had refused to admit to for several days). *The look on his face when I caught him reading* The Tempest. *Still, he admitted it, finally. . . .* She smiled a little then. He hadn't taken long to point out that her data said nothing about the fact that she devoured horse books one after another, or that he had once caught her with a long stick in hand, having an energetic swordfight with one of the trees in the vacant lot. . . .

And where is he!

She sighed and glanced down at the pages that had fallen open in her hand. One of them said:

Wizards in the closest relationships, leading toward permanent partnership, usually find that nonverbal communication becomes rare or difficult. Other conditions obtain for other species, but for human wizards, intimacy is meaningless without barriers to overcome—and to lower. Wizards usually have little need for such in the early stages of their careers. But as this situation changes, as the wizard becomes more adept at accurate description in the Speech, and therefore more adept at evaluating the people he or she works with, the wizard's mind typically adapts to the new requirements by gradually shutting out the person most—

. . . *permanent partnership?*

No. Oh, no—

Nita swallowed with a throat suddenly gone dry, and slapped the book shut. For a moment she tried to do nothing but listen to the tape. It was something of Journey's—their distinctive sweet keyboards and synthesizers, wistful, singing down toward silence. And then the vocal:

"Looking down I watch the night
running from the sun;
orphan stars and city lights
fading one by one. . . .
Oh, sweet memories, I call on you now . . ."

Of course, Nita thought, there was a lot of it going around school. Going steady, dating, pins and
rings, all the silliness. Her mother had forbidden
Nita to do any such thing, telling her she was much
too young. Nita didn't mind: it all seemed dumb to
her. Sometimes, seeing how crazed some of the
other girls her age were over the boy question, she
wondered if she was normal. She was too busy, for
one thing. She had something solider than going
steady. When you were a wizard—

—with a partner—

Oh, come on. It's not as if they're going to make
you marry him or something! Look at Tom and
Carl, they're just buddies, they work together because they enjoy doing it. . . .

But I don't want . . .

She trailed off. She didn't know what she
wanted. Nita put her head down in her hands, trying to think. No answers came: only more problems. Thoughts of Kit backing her up when she
was terrified, cheering her up when she was annoyed, Kit being the solid, reliable voice in the
other half of a spell, the presence on the far side of
the circle, matching her cadence exactly, for the
fun and the challenge of it. What's wrong with
that? What's wrong with having a best friend?

He's a boy, that's what. It's changing. *I'm* changing.

I'm scared.

She gazed up through unending night, down at

oncoming morning, and tried to work out what to do. Has he noticed this happening to him too? And suppose he starts liking someone else better than me? Will he want to keep the team going? If only I knew what he was thinking. . . .

Then she let out a sad and annoyed breath. It's probably nothing, she thought. Everything is probably fine. . . .

". . . oh, so much is wasted," sang the earphones,

> "and oh so little used!—
> but the trick of the dreamer
> is keeping yourself from the blues—"

Hah, Nita thought. I wish it were that simple. . . .

And the voice that sang cried out at her, so sudden and defiant that she sat erect with startlement—

> "Everyone's a hero
> if you want to be!
> Everyone's a prisoner
> holding their own key!
> And every step I take,
> every move I make,
> I'm always one step closer—
> I don't mind running alone!"

It was Steve Perry's fierce, clear voice, uplifted in almost angry encouragement, hitting the chorus hard. He went on, singing something about children and concrete canyons, but Nita was still full of that startlement and hardly heard. Even Dairine, she thought. There's some job out there that only she can do. . . . She had not thought of it in this light before, and the thought of Dairine as a hero staggered her, and annoyed her for a moment. Her? The runt?

But then Nita felt ashamed. What had she been herself, not more than a few months ago? Basically a coward, afraid of everything, including herself—friendless, quiet and smart but with no one to do any good by being so. Things were different now: but who was she to deny Dairine her chance at being more than she had been? *And every step I take, every move I make, I'm always one step closer.* . . .

And if *she* can do that, Nita thought after a moment, I can sure ask him what he thinks about things—

A sudden movement off to one side brought Nita's head around with a snap. In utter silence, silvery-white dust was kicking up in a vague pale cloud from where a tall man in a polo shirt and shorts was standing. Tom bounced over to where Nita sat, being careful of his footing. Nita admired the way he bounced: he had obviously had a lot of practice at the kangaroo hop that works well in low gravities.

He paused not too far from Nita to let her shield-spell recognize his and allow it to infringe, then sat down beside Nita on the boulder, casting an analytical eye over her spell diagram. "Very neat," he said. "Nice structure. Carl has been contaminating you, I see."

"Thanks."

"Kit just called me," Tom said, brushing dust off himself. "He'll be up in a few . . . he's just settling things with his folks. I'm going to be talking to them later." Tom smiled wearily. "This seems to be my night."

"Yeah."

More silverdust kicked up, closer and to the right. There was Kit, with his knapsack over his back and Picchu on one shoulder. "All set," he said to Tom. He looked at Nita and said, "They hollered a lot. But I think my dad is proud. Mom seems pretty calm about it." Then he laughed, a little wickedly. "My sisters are in shock."

"Can't say that I blame them."

Nita got up, dusting herself off. "Okay," Tom said. "I wanted to see you two off up here, because there's data you'll need that your parents don't. Something major is going on out there. Dairine is not going to run into just some bunch of lackeys for the Lone Power out there. That one Itself is after her. But I have no indication why. And Its power is oddly veiled, at the moment—concentrated, and hidden. I don't think this manifestation of the Lone Power is going to be as obvious as it has recently. So find Dairine, and look carefully at the situation. If it looks like she needs to be where she is, stay with her and do what you can for her."

He paused. "But you are going to have to be very careful. The Lone One won't mind distracting her by striking at you two . . . or using her danger to sucker you into pulling her out of the problem she's intended to correct. Use your judgment. Save her if you can."

"And if we can't?" Kit said.

Tom looked at him sadly. "See that the job gets done," he said, "whatever it is."

They were both quiet.

"There's no telling what the stakes are on this one," Tom said. "The looks of the situation may be deceiving . . . probably will. Can you take this job and do it? Don't go if you can't. If either of you isn't sure you can depend on yourself, or on the both of you, I don't want you in this. Too much can go wrong."

Kit looked at Nita, then back at Tom. "It's cool," he said.

Nita nodded. Tom looked at her.

"I know," he said. "You're upset about her. All right . . . you'll have a while to shake down, while you chase her. Meantime, Carl and I have sent word ahead through the Network, so that a lot of people will be expecting you." He smiled. "You're going to find that the way wizards have to behave on Earth is the exception rather than the rule. Most of the major law-enforcement bodies in this part of the Galaxy routinely call wizards in for consultations, and they owe us a lot of favors. So don't be afraid to ask the authorities wherever you go for help. Odds are you'll get it."

"Okay."

"So get out of here. And good hunting."

"Thanks."

"Come here, bird," Tom said to Picchu. Nita looked up in surprise, expecting an explosion: Picchu did not take orders. She was surprised to see the macaw clamber up onto Tom's arm and reach up to nibble his ear. Tom scratched her in the good place, on the back of the head, and she went vague in the eyes for a couple of minutes, then ruffled the neck feathers up and shook herself. "You be careful," Tom said.

"I'll be fine," Picchu said, sounding cranky.

Nita repacked her knapsack, slung it on, and flipped her manual open to the marked pages with the verbal supplement for the transit spell as Tom passed Peach back to Kit. She caught Kit's eye, stepped into the circle at the same time he did. Tom backed away. Slowly, and in unison, they began to read, and the air trapped in their shield-

spells began to sing the note ears sing in silence . . .

As the spell threw them out of the Solar System,
Nita wondered whether she would ever see it
again. . . .

Uplink

PLA1ETARY H1STOR1 (p1ge 3 o1116)   HE1P11/1111111

11111111111111111111111111111111111111111111111111111
11111111111111111111111111111111111111111111111111111
11111111111111111111111111111111111111111111111111111
11111111111111111111111111111111111111111111111111111
11111111111111111111111111111111111111111111111111111
11111111111111111111111111111111111111111111111111111
11111111111111111111111111111111111111111111111111111
11111111111111111111111111111111111111111111111111111
11111111111111111111111111111111111111111111111111111
11111111111111111111111111111111111111111111111111111
11111111111111111111111111111111111111111111111111111
11111111111111111111111111111111111111111111111111111
11111111111111111111111111111111111111111111111111111
11111111111111111111111111111111111111111111111111111
11111111111111111111111111111111111111111111111111111

★ 153 ★

"Dead," Dairine whispered. "I'm dead for sure."

"Input error," said the computer, sounding quite calm.

Dairine's heart leapt. "Are you busted?!" she cried.

"Syntax error 24," said the computer, "rephrase for—"

"You can take your syntax errors and . . . never mind!" Dairine said. "What's wrong with you? Diagnostic!"

"External input," said the computer. "Nontypical."

"What is it? Some kind of broadcast?"

"Negative. Local."

It happened right after it linked to the geothermal power, Dairine thought. "Check your link to the planet," she said.

"Affirmative. Positive identification. External input. Planetary source."

"Are there people here?" Dairine said, looking around hurriedly.

"Negative." The computer's screen kept filling up with 1's, clearing itself, filling with 1's again.

She held still and forced herself to take a deep breath, and another. The computer wasn't broken, nothing horrible had happened. Yet. "Can you get rid of all those ones?" she said to the computer.

"Affirmative."

The screen steadied down to the last page she had been looking at. Dairine stared at it.

This unique structure becomes more interesting when considering the physical nature of the layering. Some 92% of the layers consist of chemically pure silicon, predisposing the aggregate to electroconductive activity in the presence of light or under certain other conditions. This effect is likely to be enhanced in some areas by the tendency of silicon to superconduct at surface temperatures below 200K. There is also a possibility that semiorganic life of a "monocellular" nature will have arisen in symbiosis either with the silicon layers or their associated "doping" layers, producing—

Dairine sat there and began to tremble. It's the planet, she thought. Silicon. And trace elements, put down in layers. And cold to make it semiconduct—

"It's the planet!" she shouted at the computer. "This whole flat part here is *one big semiconductor chip*, a computer chip! It's *alive*! Send it something! Send it some 1's!"

The computer flickered through several menu screens and began filling with 1's again. Dairine rolled from her sitting position into a kneeling one, rocking back and forth with anxiety and delight. She had to be right, she had to. One huge chip, like a computer motherboard a thousand miles square. And some kind of small one-celled—if that was the right word—one-celled organism living with it. Something silicon-based, that could etch pathways in it—pathways that electricity could run along, that data could be stored in. How many years had this chip been laying itself down in the silence, she

★ 155 ★

wondered? Volcanoes erupting chemically pure silicon and trace elements that glazed themselves into vast reaches of chip-surface as soon as they touched the planet: and farther down, in the molten warmth of the planet's own geothermal heat, the little silicon-based "bacteria" that had wound themselves together out of some kind of analogue to DNA. Maybe they were more like amoebas than bacteria now: etching their way along through the layers of silicon and cadmium and other elements, getting their food, their energy, from breaking the compounds' chemical bonds, the same way carbon-based life gets it from breaking down complex proteins into simpler ones.

It was likely enough. She would check it with the manual. But for now, the result of this weird bit of evolution was all that really mattered. The chip was *awake*. With this much surface area—endless thousands of square miles, all full of energy, and connections and interconnections, millions of times more connections than there were in a human brain—how could it *not* have waked up? But there was nowhere for it to get data from that she could see, no way for it to contact the outside world. It was trapped. The 1's, the basic binary code for "on" used by all computers from the simplest to the most complex, were a scream for help, a sudden realization that something else existed in the world, and a crying out to it. Even as she looked down at the screen and watched what the computer was doing, the stream of 1's became a little less frantic. 111111111, said her own machine. *111111111,* said the planet.

"Give it an arithmetic series," Dairine whispered.

1, said her computer. 11. 111. 1111. 11111.

1. 11. 111. 1111. 11111.

"Try a geometric."

1. 11. 1111. 11111111. 1111111111111111.

1. 11. 1111. 11111111—

"Oh, it's got it," Dairine said, bouncing and still hugging herself. "I think. It's hard to tell if it's just repeating. Try a square series."

11. 1111. 1111111111111111—

111. 111111111. 111111111111111111111111111—

It had replied with a cube series. It knew, it *knew*! "Can you teach it binary?" Dairine said, breathless.

"Affirmative." 1. 10. 11. 100. 101—

Things started to move fast, the screen filling with characters, clearing itself, filling again as the computers counted at each other. Dairine was far gone in wonder and confusion. What to teach it next? It was like trying to communicate with someone who had been locked in a dark, soundless box all his life. . . . "Is it taking the data?"

"Affirmative. Writing to permanent memory."

Dairine nodded, thinking hard. Apparently the huge chip was engraving the binary code permanently into itself: that would include codes for letters and numbers as well. But what good's that gonna do? It doesn't have any experiences to make words out of, no reason to put letters together to make the words in the first place. . . . It was like it had been for Helen Keller, Dairine thought: but at least Helen had had the senses of touch and taste, so that she could feel the water poured into her hand while her teacher drummed the touch-code for *water* into it. It has no senses. If it did—

"Can you hook it into your sensors?" she said to the computer.

The computer hesitated. It had never done such a thing before: and when it spoke again, its syntax was peculiar—more fluid than she was used to. "High probability of causing damage to the corresponding computer due to too great a level of complexity," it said.

Dairine breathed out, annoyed, but had to agree. Anything able to sense events happening forty trillion miles away, no matter how it managed it, was certainly too complex to hook directly to this poor creature right now. And another thought occurred to her, and her heart beat very fast. Not sensors, then. Senses. "Can you hook *me* to it?" she said.

This time the hesitation was even longer, and Dairine stared at the computer, half expecting it to make an expression at her. It didn't, but the speech of its response was slow. "Affirmative," it said. "Triple confirmation of intent required."

"I tell you three times," Dairine said. "Hook it to

me. Tell me what to do. It has to get some better idea of what's going on out here or it'll go crazy!"

"Direct physical contact with surface," the computer said. It sounded reluctant.

Dairine dusted her hands off and put them flat on the glassy ground.

She was about to open her mouth to tell the computer to go ahead, do what it was going to: but she never got the chance. The instantaneous jolt went right through her with exactly the same painless grabbing and shaking she had felt when she was seven and had put a bobby pin in the electric socket. She convulsed, all over: her head jerked up and snapped back and she froze, unable even to blink, staring up into the golden-veiled blaze of the barred spiral, staring at it till each slight twitch of her eyes left jittering purple-green afterimages to right and left of it; and somewhere inside her, as if it were another mind speaking, she could hear her computer crying *1100100101111000010! 1100100 1011110000100!* at the frantic silence that listened. *Light, light, light—*

And the reply, she heard that too: a long, crazed string of binary that made no sense to her, but needed to make none. Joy, it was simply joy, joy at discovering *meaning*: joy so intense that all her muscles jumped in reaction, breaking her out of the connection and flinging her facedown on the glazed ground. The connection reestablished itself and Dairine's mind fell down into turmoil. She couldn't think straight: caught between the two computers—for under the swift tutelage of her own, the great glassy plain was now beginning truly to function as one—she felt the contents of her brain being twinned, and the extra copy dumped out into endless empty memory and stored, in a rush of images, ideas, occurrences, communications, theories and raw sensations. She knew it took only a short time: but it seemed to go on forever, and all her senses throbbed like aching teeth at being desperately and delightedly used and used and used again to sense this moment, this everchanging *now*. Dairine thought she would never perceive anything as completely again as she was seeing and feeling the green-and-gold-shaded piece of silicon aggregate she lay on, with the four crumbs from her sandwich lying half an inch from her eye. She felt sure she would be able to describe the shape of those crumbs and the precise pattern of the dappling in the silicon on her deathbed. If she survived this to have one.

Finally it stopped. Groaning softly, Dairine levered herself up and stared around her. The computer was sitting there innocently, its screen showing the main "Manual" menu. "How is it?" Dairine said, and then sighed and got ready to rephrase herself.

"Considerably augmented," said the computer.

Dairine stared at it.

"Is it just me," she said, "or do you sound smarter than you have been?"

"That calls for a value judgment," said the computer.

Dairine opened her mouth, then closed it again. "I guess it does," she said. "You weren't just acting as conduit all through that, were you? You expanded your syntax to include mine."

"You got it," said the computer.

Dairine took a moment to sit up. Before this, she'd thought she would love having the computer be a little more flexible. Now she was having second thoughts. "How's our friend doing?"

"Assimilating the new data and self-programming. Its present running state has analogues to trance or dream states in humans."

Dairine instantly wished it hadn't said that. What time was it at home? How long had she been running? How long had that last longest jump taken, if it had in fact taken any time at all? All she knew was that she was deadly tired.

"Update," said the computer. "It is requesting more data."

"On what?"

"No specific request. It simply desires more."

"I'm fresh out," Dairine said, and yawned. Then she looked at the computer again. "No, I'm not. Give it what *you've* got."

"Repeat and clarify?" said the computer, sounding slightly unnerved.

"Give it what you've got. All the information about planets and species and history and all the rest of it. Give it the magic!"

The computer said nothing.

Dairine sat up straight. "Go on," she said.

No reply.

"Is there some rule that says you shouldn't?"

"Yes," said the computer slowly, "but this edition of the software contains the authorization-override function."

"Good," Dairine said, none too sure of what this meant, except that it sounded promising. "I'm overriding. Give it what you've got."

The screen lit up with a block of text, in binary, quite small and neat, and Dairine immediately thought of the Oath in Nita's manual.

The screen blanked, then filled with another brief stream of binary. That blanked in turn, and screenful after screenful of 1's and 0's followed, each flickering out of existence almost as quickly as it appeared.

Dairine got up and stretched, and walked back and forth for a few minutes to work the kinks out of her muscles. She ached all over, as she had after the bobby pin incident, and her stomach growled at her again: a bologna sandwich and a half was not enough to satisfy her after the kind of day she had had. If it was even the same day. At least I have a while before the BEMs show up, she thought. Maybe our new friend here can be of some kind of help. . . . As she looked out across the dappled-silvery plain, there was a bloom of soft crimson light at one side of it. Dairine held still to watch the sun rise. It was a fat red star, far along in its lifetime—so far along, so cool, that there was water vapor in its atmosphere, and even in the vacuum of space it hung in a softly glowing rose-colored haze, like an earthly summer sunset. It climbed the sky swiftly, and Dairine watched it in silence. Quite a day, she thought. But whether it's morning here or not, I need a nap.

She turned around and started to head back toward the computer—and froze.

One patch of the surface was moving. Something underneath it was humping upward, and cracks appeared in the perfect smoothness. There was no sound, of course, since Dairine's air supply was nowhere near the spot; the cracks webbed outward in total silence.

And then the crust cracked upward in jagged pieces, and the something underneath pushed through and up and out. Bits of silica glass fell slowly in the light gravity and bounced or shattered in a snow of splinters around the rounded shape that stood there. *Stood* was the right word: for it had legs, though short stumpy ones, as if a toy tank had thrown away its treads and grown limbs instead. It shook itself, the rounded, glassy, glittering thing, and walked over to Dairine and through her shields with a gait like a centipede's or a clockwork toy's; and it looked up at her, if something like a turtle with no head can be said to look up.

"Light," it croaked, in a passable imitation of the computer's voice, and bumped against her shin, and rested there.

It was too much. Dairine sat down where she was and looked at the computer. "I can't cope," she said.

The computer had no reply for this.

"I can't," she said. "Make me some more air, please, and call me if they start chasing us again."

"No problem," said the computer.

She lay down on the smooth glassy ground, gazing at the rounded, glittery thing that stood on its fourteen stumpy legs and gazed back at her. No more than six breaths later she was asleep.

So she did not see, an hour and a half later, when the sun, at its meridian, began to pucker and twist out of shape, and for the best part of the hour lost half of itself, and shone only feebly, warped and dimmed. Her companion saw it, and said to the computer:

"What?"

"Darkness," said the computer: and nothing more.

Reserved Words

They got to Rirhath B early in the evening, arriving at the Crossings just after suns' set and just as the sky was clearing. Nita and Kit stood there in the Nontypical Transit area for a few moments, staring up at the ceiling like the rankest tourists. Picchu sat on Kit's shoulder, completely unruffled, and ignored everything with yawning scorn, though the view through the now-clear ceiling was worth seeing.

"My brains are rattled," Kit said, breathing hard. "I need a minute." So did Nita, and she felt vaguely relieved that Kit had said something about it first: so she just nodded, and craned her neck, and stared up. The view was worth looking at—this sudden revelation of Rirhath's sky, a glorious concatenation of short-term variable stars swelling and shrinking like living things that breathed and whose hearts beat fire. All over the Crossings, people of every species passing through were pausing, looking up at the same sight, and admiring the completeness with which a perfectly solid-seeming ceiling now seemed to have gone away. Others, travelers who had seen it all before or were just too tired to care, went on about their business and didn't bother to look.

"We only have a couple of days," Picchu said, chewing on the collar of Kit's shirt.

"Peach," Nita said, "shut your face. You better?" she said to Kit.

"Yeah," he said. "You?"

"I was dizzy. It's okay now."

"Super." He flipped through his manual, open in his hand, and came up with a map of the Crossings. "What do we need to find?"

"Stationmaster's office."

"Right."

They checked out of Nontypical Transit, leaving their origin-and-destination information with the computer at the entrance, and set out across the expanse of the terminal floor, looking around them in calm wonder: for though neither of them had ever been there, both had read enough about the Crossings in their manuals to know what to expect. They knew there had been a time when the Crossings itself was only a reed hut by a riverside, and the single worldgate nearby only a muddy spot in a cave that the first Master stumbled upon by accident, and claimed for its heirs (after waiting several years on Ererikh for the gate to reverse phase so that he could get home). Now, a couple of thousand years' worth of technology later, worldgates were generated here at the drop of a whim, and the Stationmaster regulated interstellar commerce and transportation via worldgating for the entire Sagittarius Arm.

Its office was not off in some sheltered spot away from the craziness, but out in the very middle of the station floor: that being the spot where the hut had been, twenty-four hundred and thirty years before. It was only a single modest kiosk of tubular bluesteel, with a desk behind it, and at the desk, hung up in a rack that looked like a large stepstool, was a single Rirhait, banging busily on a computer terminal keypad and making small noises to itself as it worked.

Nita and Kit stopped in front of the desk, and the Rirhait looked up at them. Or more or less up: some of its stalked eyes looked down instead, and a few peered from the sides. It stopped typing. "Well?" it said, scratchy-voiced—understandable, Nita thought, when you've got a gullet full of sand.

"You're the Stationmaster?" Kit said.

"Yes," said the Rirhait, and the fact that it said nothing else, but looked at Kit hungrily, with its scissory mandibles working, made Nita twitch a little.

"We are on errantry, and we greet you," Nita said: the standard self-introduction of a wizard on business. *Sir* or *Madam,* one normally added, but Nita wasn't sure which the Master was, or even if either term applied.

"That too?" said the Master, looking at Picchu.

"Yes, *that,*" said Peach, all scorn.

"Well, it's about time you people got here," said the Master, and left off what it was doing, standing up. "Standing" was an approximation: a Rirhait is shaped more like a centipede than anything else, so that when it got off its rack and came out from behind the desk, its long, shiny silver-blue body only stood a foot or so off the ground, and all its eyes looked up at them together. "We had more of an untidiness here this afternoon than we've had for a greatyear past, and I'll be glad to see the end of it."

Nita began to sweat. "The wizard who came through here earlier was on Ordeal," Kit said. "We'll need your help to find the spot from which she went farther on, so that we can track her: there are too many other worldgates here, and they're confusing the trail."

"She didn't cause any trouble, did she?" Nita said.

"Trouble?" said the Stationmaster, and led them off across the bright floor, and showed them the place where several large pieces of the ceiling had been shot down. "Trouble?" it said, pointing out the places where the floors were melted, indicating the blaster scars in the kiosks, and the large cordoned-off area where maintenance people of various species were scraping and scrubbing coffee ground–smelling residue off the floor. "Oh, no trouble. Not really."

Picchu began to laugh, a wicked and appreciative sound.

Nita blushed ferociously and didn't say anything for several minutes. The Rirhait led them off to another area of the floor which was closed in on itself by an arrangement of bluesteel kiosks. This was Crossings security; various desks stood about inside it, with creatures of several species working at them. The Master led them to one of the unoccupied desks, a low flat table full of incomprehensible equipment. "Here," it said, and reared up on its back ten legs to touch the machinery in several places.

Small and clear, an image appeared above the table: remote, but equally clear, sound accompanied it. Nita and Kit found themselves looking at the Crossroads equivalent of a videotape, but in three dimensions, with neat alien characters burning in the lower corner of it to show the time and location at which the recording was made. They watched a group of toadlike BEMs make their way across the terminal floor, spot Dairine, head off in pursuit. They watched Dairine deal with the deinonychus, and afterward with the BEM that grabbed her. Nita gulped.

"They look like Satrachi," Kit said, astonishingly cool-voiced.

Nita's eyebrows went up. Alien species were her specialty: evidently Kit had been doing some extra research. "They are, as far as we can tell," said the Master. "The one of them whom we have in custody has valid Satra identification."

"We'll need to see this person, then," Nita said. The tape ran: Nita watched Dairine's dive into the bar, and from another camera angle, her sister's reemergence into the terminal and dash into the rest room. Nita groaned, recognizing the room by the symbol on its door as a spawning room for any one of several species that gave birth to their young on the average of once every few days, and were likely to be caught short while traveling on business. Nita hoped that Dairine hadn't introduced one of the species involved to a completely new kind of birth trauma.

"That was the spot she left from?"

"Yes, Emissary." It was the first time Nita had ever been formally called by one of the twenty or so titles commonly used for wizards, but she was too busy now to enjoy it. She glanced at Kit. He was frowning at the image hanging in the air: finally his concentration broke and he glanced at her.

"Well?" he said. "You want the Satrachi?"

"I'd better," she said, though she very much wanted not to—the looks of the Satrachi gave her the creeps. But dealing with live things was her department: the handling of machinery and inanimate objects was Kit's. "You go ahead and check the room out. Stationmaster, can you have someone show me where it's being held?"

"Step on that square there," said the Master, pointing one eye at a spot on the floor: "it's direct transit to Holding. Emissary, I'll show you to the room in question. . . ."

Nita stepped on the block quickly before she would have time to change her mind.

Fifteen minutes with it told her all she needed to know: the Satra was a dupe, it and its friends—a small paramilitary club—deluded into pursuing Dairine by some agent of the Lone One. It's the usual thing, she thought as she headed back to Kit and the Stationmaster. The Power never comes out in the open if it can find some way to make someone else do Its dirty work. Preferably an innocent: that way it's more of a slap in the Bright Powers' face. Unusual, though, that it used a whole group this time. Normally it's hard to keep that subtle a grip on a whole group's mind: one of them slips free, or perceives it as control . . . and when that happens, odds are that the whole group is useless for Its purposes.

She strolled among aliens and their luggage and

finally came to the little Grand Central–size alcove where Dairine's rest room was. Its door was frozen in the dilated mode. Nita slipped in and found Kit and Picchu and the Master off to one side, examining one particular birthing-booth. It seemed to have had its door burned off, and the back of the booth was blistered and pocked with an ugly rash of blaster scars.

For a good second or so her breath refused to come. "She jumped after *that*?" Nita finally managed to say.

Kit looked over his shoulder at her. "Neets, relax, there are no bloodstains."

"There wouldn't be, with blasters," Nita said. "They cauterize."

"Any really big wound would spurt anyway," Kit said, straightening up and starting to page through his manual. "I think they missed her. The tiles don't remember her screaming, and not even Dairine's *that* stoic." He kept turning over pages.

"How far did she go?"

"A long jump," Kit said. "Multistage, from the feel of it. They must have freaked her out pretty good." He looked up. "That computer she's got leaves a definite sense of what it's been doing behind it. Can you feel it?"

Nita let her eyes go unfocused for a moment and blanked her mind out, as she might do to hear the thinking of some particularly quiet tree. Some residue of Dairine's emotion still hung about the strings in the space-time configuration of the area, like tatters on a barbed-wire fence: fear and defiance, all tangled up together; and alongside her tatters, others, ordered and regular, a weave less vivid and complex in different ways. "It feels alive," Nita said to Kit after a while. "Do computers usually feel that way?"

"I don't know," Kit said, sounding annoyed. "I never tried feeling one before this. . . . You got your widget?" he said. "We're gonna need it to catch up with her and her friends."

"Yeah." She unslung her pack and started rummaging for the gimbal.

"Well, I have things to do," said the Master. "If you need anything, ask one of the security people, they're all over." And without staying for farewells, it went flowing out the door in a hundred-legged scurry.

Nita glanced after it, then back at Kit, and shrugged. "Here," she said, and tossed him the gimbal. "Which spell are you thinking of using?"

"That dislocator on page 1160."

She got out her own manual and found the page. "That's awful long-range, isn't it? Her next jump must have been shorter than that."

"Yeah, but Neets, who wants to leapfrog one step behind the things that are chasing her! We want *them*, right now—we want them off her rear end, so she can do whatever it is she needs to do with-

★ 173 ★

out interference." He looked grim. "And when we find 'em—"

Nita sighed. "Forget it," she said, "they're dupes."

Kit looked up at her while getting a grease pencil out of his pack. "It suckered them in?"

She filled him in on what the Satrachi had told her as Kit got down on the tiles and began drawing their transit circle. Kit sighed a little. "I was hoping it was some of the Lone One's own people," he said, "so we could just trash 'em and not feel guilty."

Nita had to smile a little at that. Picchu climbed down from the partition between the booths, where he had been sitting, and clambered onto Nita's shoulder. "Get mine right," she said to Kit. "I don't want to come out the other side of this transit with fur."

Kit shot a look at Picchu, and didn't need to comment; Nita could imagine what he was thinking. "Come sit over here, then, if you're so worried," he said.

To Nita's amusement Peach did just that, climbing backward down her arm and over onto Kit's back, where she peered over his shoulder. "Not bad," she said, looking at the diagram.

Kit ignored this. "So make yourself useful. Is anything bad going to happen to us?"

"Of course it is," Picchu said.

"You might be more specific."

"And I might not need to. The Power that invented death is going to be on your tails shortly.

Our tails," she added, looking over her shoulder at the splendid three-foot sweep of scarlet feathers behind her. "Even you two should be able to see that coming."

Kit changed position suddenly, and Picchu scrabbled for balance, flapping her wings and swearing. "Like you should have seen that?"

Nita grinned a little, then let it go: her mind was back on the train of thought she had been playing with out in the terminal. "I was wondering about that, a while back," she said to Kit. "It invented death, when things were first started. But that wasn't enough for It. It had to get people to buy into death—not just the dying itself: the *fear* of it."

Kit nodded. "But a lot of species have opted out, one way or another. I mean, we're scared to die. But we still suspect there are reasons *not* to be scared. A lot of people do. Its hold isn't complete anymore."

"I know. Kit, do you think—Tom said something was about to 'tip over.' Some major change. Do you think what he meant was that the Lone One was about to lose *completely* somewhere?"

"He always said," Kit said, "that what happens one place, spreads everyplace else. Everything affects everything, sooner or later. The manual says so too. A few times."

Nita nodded, thinking how unusual it was for the manual to repeat itself about anything. "And the pattern started shifting, a couple thousand years ago," Kit said. "The Lone Power *had* always won completely before. Then It started having wins taken away from It after the fact."

Kit looked reflective. "If somewhere or other, It's about to *lose*—right from the start . . ."

Nita looked at him sidewise. "Then It starts losing at home, too, in all the little daily battles. Eventually."

Kit nodded. "Dairine," he said.

Nita shook her head, still having trouble believing it—but having to admit the likelihood. Somehow, her sister had a chance of actually defeating the Lone Power. She *must* have a chance: It wouldn't be wasting energy on her otherwise. "Why her?" Nita said softly.

"Why *you*?" said Picchu, cranky. "What makes either of you so special, that you can even come away from an encounter with That alive? Don't flatter yourself: It's eaten stars and seduced whole civilizations in Its time. You were simply exactly the right raw material for that particular situation to use to save Itself."

"I didn't mean that, I guess," she said. "I meant, why now? The Lone Power has been pulling this kind of stunt on planets for as long as intelligence has been evolving. It comes in, It tries to get people to accept entropy willingly, and then It bugs off and leaves them to make themselves more miserable than even It could do if It worked at it. Fine.

But now all of a sudden It can be beaten. How come?"

Picchu began chewing on Kit's top button. "You know," she said, "that's part of the answer. Granted, It's immortal. But It doesn't have infinite power. It's peer to all the Powers, but not to That in Which they move. And even an immortal can get tired."

Nita thought about that. Five billion years, maybe ten, of constant strife, of incomplete victories, of rage and frustration—and yes, loneliness: for the Lone One, she had discovered to her shock, was ambivalent about Its role—after all that, surely one might not be as strong as one had been at the start of things. . . .

Kit got the button out of Picchu's mouth, and was nipped for his trouble. "So, after all these near losses, It's tired enough to be beaten outright?"

Picchu got cranky again. "Of course! It was *that* tired long ago. The Powers wouldn't need Dairine for just that. They could do it Themselves, or with the help of older wizards. But haven't you got it through your head? They can't want to just *beat* the Lone One. They must think there's a better option."

Nita looked at Picchu, feeling half frightened. "They want It to *surrender*," she said.

"I think so," said Picchu. "I suspect They think she could get the Lone One to give in and come back to Its old allegiance. If It does that . . . the effect spreads. Slowly. But it spreads everywhere."

Picchu climbed down off Kit's shoulder and pigeon-toed across the floor, heading for a receptacle with some water in it. Kit and Nita both sat silent. The possibility seemed a long way from coming true. A world in which the universe's falling into entropy slowly stopped, affecting people's relationships with one another, a world gradually losing the fear of death, a world losing hatred, losing terror, losing evil itself . . . it was ridiculous, impossible, too much to hope for. But still, Nita thought, if there was any chance at all . . . ! ". . . On the news last night," Kit said, "did you see that thing about the car in Northern Ireland?"

"No."

"They hijack cars over there sometimes, as a protest," he said. "One side or the other." There was something about his voice that made Nita look at him hard. "Sometimes they set the cars on fire after they hijack them." Kit sat looking in front of him at nothing in particular, looking tired. "You know the kind of wire screen you get for station wagons, so that your dog can be in the back and not get into everything?"

"Yeah."

"Someone hijacked a car with one of those in it, the other night. With the dog in it, in the back. Then they set the car on fire. With the dog in it."

Nita went ashen. Kit just kept looking at nothing in particular, and she knew what he was thinking of: Ponch, in Kit's dad's station wagon, lying around in the back too contented and lazy even to try to get into the grocery bags all around him. And someone coming up to the car—"Neets," Kit said, after a while, "Bad enough that they kill children, and grown-ups, and don't even care. But the poor dogs too—if we really have a chance to stop that kind of thing, I'll do . . . whatever. I don't care. Anything."

She looked at him. *"Anything?"*

He was quiet for a long time. "Yeah."

Eventually she nodded. "Me too."

"I know," he said.

She looked at him in surprise. "Well, look at what you did with the whales," he said.

Nita's mouth was very dry. She tried to swallow. It didn't work.

"I mean, you did that already. That's what it was about. The Power got redeemed, a little: we know that much. Or at least It got the option to change. You did it for *that*. You almost got yourself killed, and you knew that might happen, and you did it anyway. Oh, I know you did it for me, some." He said this as if it were unimportant. "I was in trouble, you got me out of it. But mostly you did it to have things in the world be safe, and work."

She nodded, completely unable to speak.

"It seems like the least I can do," he said, and went no further, as if Nita should know perfectly well what he meant.

"Kit," she said.

"Look, I mean, I don't know if I can be that brave, but—"

"Kit, shut up."

He shut, rather astonished.

I'm always one step closer, sang memory at her from the Moon. "Look," she said, "I didn't do it for you 'some.' I did it for you 'pretty much.'"

Kit looked at her with an expression that at first made Nita think Kit thought she was angry with him. But then it became plain that he was embarrassed too. "Well," he said, "okay. I—thought maybe you did. But I didn't want to say anything because I didn't know for sure. And I would have felt real stupid if I was wrong." He had been looking away. Now he looked at her. "So?"

"So," and her voice stuck again, and she had to clear her throat to unstick it. "I *like* you, that's all. A lot. And if you start liking somebody that much, well, I still want to keep the team going. If you do. That's all."

He didn't say anything. Nita stood there burning in a torment of embarrassment and anger at herself.

"Neets. Cut me some slack. You're my best friend."

Her head snapped up. ". . . I thought it was Richie Sussman."

Kit shrugged. "We just play pool a lot. But it's the truth." He looked at her. "Isn't it true for you?"

"Yeah, but—"

"So why does that have to change? Look, we've got junk to do. Let's shake on it. We'll be best friends forever. And a team."

He said it so casually. But then that was how Kit did things: the only thing that wasn't casual was the way he worked to do what he said he would. "What if something happens?" Nita said. "What if—"

Kit finished one symbol inside the circle, shut the book, and stood up. "Look," he said, "something always happens. You still have to promise stuff anyway. If you have to work to make the promises true . . ." He shrugged, hefted the manual. "It's like a spell. You have to say the words every time you want the results. Neets, come on. Shake on it."

They shook on it. Nita felt oddly light, as if her knapsack had been full of rocks and someone had come up behind her and dumped them out.

"Okay," Kit said. "Peach, where—good Lord."

Picchu was sitting in the water receptacle on the floor, flapping around and showering everything within range. "Do you mean I'm going to have to go halfway across the Galaxy with a soggy bird sitting on me?" Kit said. "No way. Neets, it's your turn to carry her."

"You're getting a lot like Tom," said Picchu.

"Thanks!"

"That wasn't intended as a compliment."

Peach shook her feathers, scattering water. "Stop

★ 181 ★

your complaining," she said to Kit. "The Powers only know when I'm going to have another chance for a bath." She stepped out of the low basin and shook herself again all over.

Nita wiped a drop out of her eye. "Come on," she said, and got Peach off the edge of the basin. "Kit, we set?"

"Yup. You want to do a defense spell, do it now. Peach? Any bad feelings?"

"All of them," Picchu said, "but nothing specific. Let's go."

They all three got into the circle. Kit knotted it closed with the figure-eight wizard's knot, dropped the gimbal into the circle on the spot marked out for it, then picked up his manual and began to read. Nita silently recited her favorite shieldspell, the one that could stop anything from a thrown punch to an ICBM, and for safety's sake set it at ICBM level. Then she got her own manual open and caught up with Kit. The air began to sing the note ears sing in silence; the air pushed in harder and harder around them, Nita's ears popped, and the spell took hold and threw them off the planet— not before Nita saw a portly Me!thai gentleman peek in the door to see if it was safe to come in and have his child. . . .

There was a long, long darkness between the world winking out and flashing back into existence again. Nita could never remember its having taken so long before—but then the jump from Earth to

Rirhath had been a short one, no more than fifteen or twenty light-years. She held her breath and maintained control, even while the back of her brain was screaming frantically, *He made a mistake in the spell somewhere, you distracted him and he misspelled something else: you're stuck in this and you're never going to get out, never—*

It broke. Nita was as dizzy as she had been the last time, but she was determined not to wobble. Her ears stopped ringing as she blinked and tried to get her bearings. "Heads up, Neets," Kit was saying.

It was dark. They stood on some barren unlit moon out in the middle of space. Nothing was in the sky but unfamiliar stars and the flaming, motionless curtain of an emission nebula, flung across the darkness like a transparent gauze burning in hydrogen red and oxygen blue. Kit pointed toward the horizon where the nebula dipped lowest. Amid a clutter of equipment and portable shelters of some kind, there stood a small crowd of Satrachi. They had apparently not noticed their pursuers' appearance.

"Right," Nita said. "Let's do this—"

"Move us!" Picchu screeched. *"Do it now!"*

Kit's eyes widened. He started rereading the spell, changing the end coordinates by a significant amount. Peach was still flapping her wings and screaming. "No, that's not far enough—"

Nita snatched the gimbal up from the ground

and tied it into her shieldspell. Can it take the strain of two spells at once? We'll find out. It'll abort the one it can't manage, anyway. She gulped. Physical forces— She started reciting in the Speech, naming every force in the universe that she could think of, tying their names into her shield and forbidding them entrance. Can I pull this off? Is this one of the spells that has a limit on the number of added variables? Oh Lord, I hope not—

"Light," Peach was screaming at her, "light, *light!*"

Nita told the shield to be opaque—and then wondered why it wasn't, as the brightest light she had ever imagined came in through it anyway. She had been to a Shuttle launch, once, and had come to understand that sound could be a force, a thing that grabbed you from inside your chest and shook you effortlessly back and forth. Now she wondered how she had never thought that light might be able to do the same, under some circumstances. It struck her deaf and dumb and blind, and she went sprawling. Heat scorched her everywhere; she smelled the rotten-egg stink of burning hair. She clutched the gimbal: she couldn't have dropped it if she'd tried.

Much later, it seemed, it began to get dark. She opened her eyes and could not be sure, for a few minutes, that they were open, the world was so full of afterimages. But the purple curtain between her and everything else eventually went away. She and Kit and Peach were hanging suspended, weightless in empty space. At least it was empty now. There was no sign of any moonlet—only off to one side, a blinding star that slowly grew and grew and grew and grew, toward them. They were out of its range now. They had not been before.

"Didn't know the gimbal could handle both those spells," Kit said, rubbing his eyes. "Nice going."

"It won't do it twice," Nita said. There was just so much power one could milk out of a physical aid, and she had been pushing her odds even trying it once. "Where are we?"

"I haven't the faintest. Somewhere a light-month out from our original position. And those Satrachi were bait," he said. "For us. Look at it, Neets."

She looked. "I could have sworn I opaqued this shield."

"It *is* opaqued," Kit said. "But a shield doesn't usually have to put up with a nova at close range. H-bombs are about the most one can block out without leakage, if I remember."

Nita stared at the raging star, all boiling with huge twisted prominences. For all its brilliance, there was a darkness about its heart, something wrong with the light. In a short time this terrible glory would be collapsed to a pallid dwarf star, cooling slowly to a coal. She shivered: one of the oldest epithets for the Lone Power was "Starsnuffer." It blew a whole star, just to kill us, because we were going to help Dairine. . . . "Did this system have other planets?" she said.

"I don't know. I doubt It cared."

And this was what was going after her little sister.

The anger in Nita got very, very cold. "Let's go find her," she said.

Together they began to read.

Fatal Error

Dairine woke up stiff and aching all over . . . 's wrong with the bed? was her first thought: it felt like the floor. Then she opened her eyes, and found that she *was* on the floor . . . or a surface enough like one to make no difference. The cool, steady stars of space burned above her. She sat up and rubbed her sticky eyes.

I feel awful, she thought. I want a bath, I want breakfast, I want to brush my teeth! But baths and toothbrushes and any food but bologna sandwiches with mustard were all a *long* way away.

She dropped her hands into her lap, feeling slow and helpless, and looked about her. A sense of shock grew in her: all around, in what had been the absolutely smooth surface of the planet, there were great cracked holes, as if the place had had a sudden meteor shower while she was asleep. But the debris lying around wasn't the kind left by meteor strikes. "Sheesh," she muttered.

Something poked her from behind.

Dairine screamed and flung herself around. She found herself staring at the small, turtlelike glassy creature that had been the last straw the night before. It had walked into her, and was continuing to do so, its short jointed legs working busily though it was getting nowhere: like a windup toy mindlessly walking against a wall. "With," it said.

"Oh, heck," Dairine said in relief. She sagged with embarrassment. Two days ago she would have thought scorn to scream because of *anything*, up to and including Darth Vader himself . . . but the world looked a little different today.

She grabbed the steadily pedaling little thing and held it away from her to look at it. It was all made of the same silicon as the surface; the inside of its turtlish body was a complex of horizontal layers, the thickest of them about half an inch across, the thinnest visible only as tiny colored lines no thicker than a hair . . . thousands of them packed together, at times, in delicate bandings that blended into one subtle color. Dairine knew she was looking at a chip or board more complex than anything dreamed of on Earth. She could see nothing identifiable as a sensor, but it had certainly found her right away last night: so it could see. She wondered if it could hear.

"Well, how about it, small stuff?" she said. It was rather cute, after all. "Say hi."

"Hi," it said.

She put her eyebrows up, and looked over her shoulder at the computer, which was sitting where she had left it the night before. "Did you teach this guy to talk?"

"There is very little I did not teach the mind that made them," said the computer calmly.

Dairine looked around at the many, many jagged holes in the surface. "I bet. Where are they all?"

"Indeterminate. Each one began walking around the surface in a random fashion as soon as it was produced."

"Except for this one," Dairine said, and lifted the creature into her lap. It was surprisingly light. Once there, the creature stopped trying to walk, and just rested across her knees like a teatray with a domed cover on it. "Good baby," Dairine said. She touched one of the legs carefully, maneuvering the top joint gently to see how it worked. There were three joints: one ball-and-socketlike joint where it met the body, and two more spaced evenly down the leg, which was about six inches long. The legs were of the same stuff as the outer shell of the body dome: translucent, like cloudy glass, with delicate hints of color here and there. "Why didn't you go walking off with everybody else, huh?" she said as she picked it up to flip it over and examine its underside.

Its legs kicked vigorously in the air. "With," it said.

Dairine put the creature down, where it immediately walked into her again and kept walking, its legs slipping on the smooth surface.

"With, huh. Okay, okay, 'with' already." She picked it up again and put it in her lap. It stopped kicking.

She glanced up at the sky. The galaxy was rising again. For a few seconds she just held still, watching the curving fire of it. "How long is the day here?" she said.

"Seventeen hours," said the computer.

"Fast for such a big planet," she said. "Mostly light elements, though. I guess it works. How long was I asleep?"

"Fourteen hours."

Dairine made an annoyed face. There went that much of her research time. She felt fairly certain that if the BEMs didn't catch up with her shortly, someOne else would. She didn't like the thought. "I've got to get some work done," she said, and glanced down at the turtly, glassy creature in her lap. "What about you? You can't sit here all day. Neither can I."

"Hi," said the glass turtle.

She had to laugh. "Are you still talking to"—she

didn't know what to call it: she patted the glassy ground—"our friend here?"

"Yes," the computer said. "Response is slow. It is still assimilating and coordinating the data."

"Still?" Dairine let out a breath. If there was so much information in the manual functions that a computer with this much memory was still sorting it, what hope did she have of finding the information she needed in time to be able to do anything useful to the Lone One with it? She was going to have to help it along somehow. "Can you ask it to call back this little guy's friends? I want to look at them."

"Working."

Dairine stretched and considered that the next time she went out to space, she was going to plan things a little more carefully. Or stay at a hotel. Where, for example, was she going to find something to drink? She hadn't squirreled anything away in her claudication: she was going to have to find water. More to the point, there were no bathrooms here. Dairine wished heartily that she had taken time in the Crossings, or even back at Natural History, to use the facilities for something other than programming interstellar jumps. The memory of what sometimes seemed to be her mother's favorite line, "You should have gone before we left!" made her grin ruefully.

She got up to improvise what she could. Her turtle started to go with her. "No," she said, as she might have to Ponch. "Stay!" The turtle's response to this was the same as Ponch's would have been: It went after her anyway.

Dairine sighed and headed off to a little outcropping of rock about half a mile away. When she had finished, and started back to where the computer lay, she could already see small shapes moving on the horizon. She sat down with her bread and bologna, started making a sandwich, and waited for them.

Pretty soon she was knee-deep in turtles, or would have been had she been standing up. After the first few walked into her as her lapturtle had, she asked the computer to get them to hold still when they reached her. Something like two hundred of them were shortly gathered around her. They were all exact copies of her friend, even to the striations and banding inside them. She sighed a little as she looked at them.

"This isn't gonna work, you guys," she said. "There's more to life than walking around, and none of you have anything like hands. . . ."

"Hi!" said all the turtles, simultaneously. She couldn't hear the ones that were outside her bubble of air, but the ones that were inside made racket enough.

She had to laugh at that. "Look," she said to the computer, pushing her first turtle out of her lap and putting the computer there instead, "where did the mind behind these critters get the design for them?"

"Probably from one of the design templates in the "Make" utility," said the computer.

"Okay, let's get into that. If these guys are going to be the arms and legs for the mind that's running them, they need arms!"

The computer's screen flicked obediently to the opening screen for the "Make" utility. Dairine frowned at the menu for a while. The computer had a machine-assisted drafting utility: she chose that, while her turtle tried to climb back into her lap.

"No," she said. "No, honey!"

It was no use. "With!" said the turtle. "With, with, with, with—"

She laughed helplessly. "Boy, are *you* ever GIGO," she said.

"Yes," the turtle said, and sat down next to her abruptly, folding all its legs under it like a contented mechanical cat.

Dairine put her eyebrows up at that. Was that all it wanted? A name? "Gigo," she said, experimentally.

"Yes!"

It sounds happy, she thought. Can it have emotions?

"Good baby," she said, and patted it. "Good Gigo."

"Yes!" said Gigo, and "Yes!" said several of the

other turtles around, and it began to spread through the crowd to the limits of her air: "Yes, yes, yes—"

"Okay," she said, "he's good, you're all good, now put a cork in it!"

They fell silent. But there had been no mistaking the sound of joy.

"I can see I'm gonna have to find names for all of you," she said. "Can't have the whole bunch of you answering to that."

She turned her attention to the blank graphics screen. "Bring up the design that . . ." She paused. "I can't just keep banging on the ground. Does what you were talking to have a name for itself?"

"No."

Dairine sighed. "Okay, just let's call it a mother-board for the moment. Bring up the design it was using for Gigo and his buddies."

The screen flickered, showing Dairine a three-dimensional diagram, which the computer then rotated to show all the turtle's surfaces. "Good," she said. "How do I make changes?"

"The screen is touch-sensitive. Touch a line and state what you want done with it."

Dairine spent a cheerful hour or so there, pausing for bites of sandwich, as she started to redesign the turtles. She wasn't shy about it. The original design had its points, but as the mobile units of an intelligence, the turtles were sadly lacking in necessary equipment. She built several of the legs into arms, with six claws apiece at the end of them, four "fingers" and two opposable "thumbs"; this hand she attached to the arm by a ball-and-socket joint so that it could rotate completely around without having to stop. As an afterthought, she put another pair of arms on the turtle's back end, so that it wouldn't have to turn around to pick something up if it didn't want to.

She took the turtle's rather simplistic visual sensor, barely more than a photosensitive spot, and turned it into something of a cross between the human retina and a bee's faceted eye—a multiple-lensed business equally good for close work and distant vision. She placed several of these around the turtle's perimeter, and a couple on top, and then for good measure added a special-purpose lens that was actually something like a small Cassegrain telescope, focusing on a mirror-polished bit of silicon buried a ways into the turtle's "brain." She added infrared and ultraviolet sensing. Ears for sound they already had; she considered that it might be wise to give them something to hear radio with, too, but couldn't decide on which frequency to work with, and let the idea go for the moment. They could work it out themselves.

Dairine sat staring at the screen, musing. The newly awakened intelligence had made all its mobiles alike: probably because it didn't understand the concept of otherness yet. She would make them different from one another. But they were going to have to be different on the inside, too, to do any good. If some danger comes along that they have to cope with, it's no use their information processors being all the same: whatever it is could wipe them all out at once. If they're as different as they can be, they'll have a better chance of surviving.

She paused in her design to look closely at the structure of the chip layering in the turtles—not so much at what the layers were made of, but what their arrangement meant. At the molecular level she found the basic building-block of the chips, as basic as DNA in humans: not a chain molecule, but a sort of tridimensional snowflake of silicon atoms and atoms of other elements. DNA was simple beside these. Any given silicon molecule hooked with up to fourteen others, using any one of fifty different chemical compounds to do it; and every different arrangement of hookups between molecules or layers had a specific meaning, as each arrangement has in DNA. With the help of the computer she began to sort out the code buried in the interconnected snowflakes. Hours, it took her, and she was perfectly aware that even with the computer's help she couldn't hope to deal with more than the tip of this iceberg of information. Some parts of the chip structure she did manage to identify as pure data storage, others as sensor array, associative network, life support, energy management.

Dairine began devising layering arrangements different from those in the turtles. She designed creatures that would have more associative network and so could specialize in problem solving: others with more data stacks, turtles that would be good at remembering; mobiles more richly endowed with sensors, and senses, than some of the others, that would see and hear and feel most acutely. One arrangement of layers, the one that the computer identified for her as the seat of the turtles' emotions, seemed an awfully tiny thing to Dairine. She expanded it to about three times its original size, and allowed it to interconnect at will with the other associative areas, with data memory and with the senses. Finally, to every model she designed, Dairine added a great deal of latent memory area, so that each mobile would have plenty of room to store what it experienced and to process the data it accumulated.

Having done all these things, she went back to her original design and copied it several times, making a number of different "models": a large, strong one for heavy work; a small one with extra hands in various sizes, from human-hand size to tiny claws that could have done microsurgery or precision work almost on the molecular level. And she added the necessary extra sensor arrays or materials reinforcement that these changes would need to support them.

She sat back and sighed then, and unfolded her cramped legs, and reached down for her sandwich, which had gone stale on top while she worked.

"Okay," she said to the computer. "Ask the motherboard to run off a few of those and let's see what happens."

"Considerable reprogramming will be necessary," said the computer.

"I know," said Dairine, between bites of the sandwich, making a face at the taste of it. "I'm in no rush."

The computer's screen filled with binary as it began conferring with the motherboard in machine language. What do I *mean* I'm in no rush? Dairine thought, momentarily distracted while Gigo climbed into her lap again. "Did you finish that analysis run about the Lone One for me?"

"Yes," said the computer. "Do you want it displayed?"

"Yeah, please."

The binary went away from the screen, replaced by print. Dairine didn't look at it immediately. She leaned back and gazed up. The galaxy was all set but for one arm, trailing up over the far, far horizon, a hook of light. The dull red sun was following it down as if attached to the hook by an invisible string. An old, old star, Dairine thought. Not even main-sequence anymore. This could have been one of the first stars created in this universe. . . . Might have been, considering how far out this galaxy— The thought was shocked out of her.

Something other than her voice was making a sound. It was a rumbling, very low, a vibration in the surface she sat on. "What the— You feel that?" she said to the computer.

"Vibration of seismic origin," the computer said. "Intensity 2.2 Richter and increasing."

There was precious little on the planet's surface to shake. Dairine stood up, alarmed, and watched the turtles. For all their legs, they were having trouble keeping their footing on the slick surface. Gigo hooked a leg around Dairine's and steadied itself that way. "Is this gonna get worse?" Dairine said.

"Uncertain. No curve yet. Richter 3.2 and increasing. Some volcanic eruption occurring in planet's starward hemisphere."

Got to do something about their leg design if this happens a lot, Dairine thought—and then was distracted again, because something was happening to the light: It wavered oddly, dimming from the clear rose that had flooded the plain to a dark dry color like blood. She stared upward.

The sun was twisting out of shape. There was no other way to describe it. Part of its upper right-hand quarter seemed pinched on itself, warped like a round piece of paper being curled. Prominences stretched peculiarly, snapped back to tininess again: the warping worsened, until the star that had been normal and round was squeezed small, as if in a cruel fist, to a horizontal, fluctuating oval, then to a sort of tortured heart-shape, then to an oval bent the other way, leftward. Sunspots stretched like pulled taffy, oozed back to shape again, and the red light wavered and shifted like that of a candle about to be blown out in the wind.

Dairine stood with a terrible sickness at the heart of her, for this was no kind of eclipse or other astronomical event that she had ever heard of. It was as if she was seeing the laws of nature broken in front of her.

"What *is* that?" she whispered.

"Transit of systemic object across primary," said the computer. "The transiting object is a micro black hole."

Dairine sat down again, feeling the rumbling beneath her start to die away. The computer had mentioned the presence of that black hole earlier, but in the excitement she had forgotten it. "Plot me that thing's orbit," she said. "Is that going to happen every day?"

"Indeterminate. Working."

"I don't like that," said Gigo with sudden clarity.

Dairine looked over at it with surprise and pulled it into her lap. "You're not alone, small stuff," she said. "It gives me the shakes too." She sat there for a second, noticing that she was sweating. "You're getting smart, huh?" she said. "Your mom down there is beginning to sort out the words?"

"It hurts," said Gigo, sounding a little mournful.

"Hurts . . ." Dairine wasn't sure whether this was a general statement or an answer to her question. Though it could be both. A black hole in orbit in the star system would produce stresses in a planet's fabric that the planet—if it were alive, like this one—could certainly feel. Line the black hole up with its star, as it would be lined up in transit, and the tidal stresses would be that much worse. What better cause to learn to tell another person that something was hurting you? . . . Now that there was another person to tell.

Dairine patted Gigo absently. "It's all over, Gigo," she said.

"Gigo, yes."

She grinned faintly. "You really like having a name, huh?"

"A program must be given a name to be saved," Gigo said quite clearly, as if reciting from memory —but there was also slight fear in its voice, and great relief.

"Well, it's all over," Dairine said . . . while surreptitiously checking the sky to make sure. Tiny though it was—too small to see—a micro black hole was massive enough to bend light toward it. That was what had made the sun look so strange, as the gravity center of the black hole's field bent the round image of the sun forward onto itself. The realization made Dairine feel a lot better, but she didn't particularly want to see the sun do that again. She turned back to the computer. "Let's get back to work."

"Which display first," the computer said, "the

black hole's orbit or the research run on the Lone Power?"

"The orbit."

It drew it for her on the screen, a slowly moving graphic that made Dairine's insides crawl. The black hole's orbit around its primary was irregular. These transits occurred in twenty out of every thirty orbits, and in the middle five orbits the hole swung much closer to the planet and appeared to center more closely on the sun. This last one had been a grazing transit: the micro hole had only passed across the upper limb of the star. Dairine did not want to see what a dead-center transit would look like, not at all. But in the midst of her discomfort, she still found a little room to be fascinated. Apparently the black hole was the cause of the planet's many volcanoes: the tidal stresses it produced brought up molten silicon, which erupted and spread over the surface. Without the frequent passages of the hole near the planet, the millions of layers of the motherboard would never have been laid down, and it would never have reached the critical "synapse" number necessary for it to come alive. . . .

"Okay," she said. "Give me the research run, and let me know when the motherboard's ready to make some more of these guys."

"Working."

Dairine began to read, hardly aware of it when Gigo sneaked into her lap again and stared curiously at the screen. She paged past Nita's and Kit's last run-in with the Lone Power and started skimming the precis before it for common factors. Odd tales from a hundred planets flicked past her, and sweat slowly began to break out on Dairine as she realized she could not see any common factors at all. She could see no pattern in what made the Lone Power pick a specific world or group or person to attack, and no sure pattern or method for dealing with It. Some people seemed to beat the Lone One off by sheer luck. Some did *nothing* that she could see, and yet ruined Its plans utterly. One wizard on a planet of Altair had changed the whole course of his world's history by inviting a person he knew to be inhabited by the Lone One to dinner . . . and the next day, the Altairans' problem (which Dairine also did not understand except that it had something to do with the texture of their fur) simply began to clear up, apparently by itself.

"Maybe I should buy It a hot dog," Dairine muttered. That would make as much sense as most of these solutions. She was getting a feeling that there was something important about dealing with the Lone Power that the computer wasn't telling her.

She scrolled back to Nita and Kit's precis again and read it through carefully, comparing it with what she had seen them do or heard them say herself. Her conversation with Nita after she had seen her sister change back from being a whale was described in the precis as "penultimate clarification and choice." Dairine scowled. What had Nita chosen? And why? She wished she had her there to ask her . . . but no. Dairine didn't think she could cope with Nita at the moment. Her sister would certainly rip into her for doing dumb things, and Dairine wasn't in the mood . . . considering how many dumb things she *had* done in the past day and a half.

Still, Dairine thought, a little advice would come in real useful around now. . . .

"Ready," said the computer suddenly.

"Okay. Ask it to go ahead."

"Warning," the computer said. "The spell being used requires major restructuring of the substrate. Surface stability will be subject to change without notice."

"You mean I should stand back?"

"I thought that was what I said," said the computer.

Dairine made a wry face, then picked it up and started walking. "C'mon, Gigo, all you guys," she said. "Let's get out of the way."

They trooped off obediently after her. Finally, about a quarter-mile away, she stopped. "This far enough away, you think?" she said to the computer.

"Yes. Working now."

She felt a rumbling under the surface again, but this was less alarming than that caused by the transit of the black hole—a more controlled and purposeful sound. The ground where Dairine had been sitting abruptly sank in on itself, swallowing the debris caused by the breaking-out of the turtles. Then slow ripples began to travel across the surface, as it turned itself into what looked like a bubbling pot of syrup, clear in places, swirled and streaked with color in others. Heat didn't seem to be involved in the process. Dairine sat down to watch, fascinated.

"Unnamed," Gigo said next to her, "data transfer?"

Dairine looked down at the little creature. "You want to ask me a question? Sure. And I have a name, it's Dairine."

"Dairrn," it said. She chuckled a little. Dairine had never been terribly fond of her name—people tended to stumble over it. But she rather liked the way Gigo said it. "Close enough," she said. "What's up?"

"Why do you transfer data so slowly?"

That surprised her for a moment, until she considered the rate at which the computer and the motherboard had been talking: and this was in fact the motherboard she was talking to now. To something that had been taught to reckon its time in milliseconds, conversation with her must seem about as fast as watching a tree grow. "For my kind of life, I'm pretty quick," Dairine said. "It just looks slow to you."

"There is more—slowlife?"

"Lots more. In fact, you and the Apple there are about the only, uh, 'quicklife' there is, as far as I know." She paused and said, "Quick *life*, as opposed to dumb machines that are fast, but not alive."

"I see it, in the data the Lightbringer gave us," said Gigo. Dairine glanced over at the computer. "Data transfer?"

"Sure," Dairine said.

"What is the purpose of this new program run?"

Wow, its syntax is really shaping up. If this keeps up, it's gonna be smarter than me! . . . Is that a good idea? But Dairine laughed at it. It was the best idea: a supercomputer faster than a Cray, with more data in it than all the New York Public Library—what a friend to have! "When I'm gone," Dairine said, "you're going to need to be able to make your own changes in your world. So I'm making you mobiles that will be able to make the changes."

"Data transfer! Define 'gone'!"

Gigo's urgency surprised Dairine. "I can't stay here," she said. No, better simplify. "My physical presence here must terminate soon," she said. "But don't worry. You guys won't be alone."

"We will!" cried Gigo, and the whole planet through him.

"No, you won't," Dairine said. "Don't panic. Look, I'm taking care of it. You saw all the different bodies I wrote into the 'Make' program for you?

You saw how they're all structured differently on the inside? That's so they can have different personalities. There'll be lots more of you."

"How?"

Dairine hoped she could explain this properly. "You'll split yourself up," she said. "You'll copy your basic programming in a condensed form into each one of them, and then run them all separately."

There was a long, long silence. "Illegal function call," said Gigo slowly.

"It's not. Believe me. It sounds like it, but it works just fine for all the slowlife . . . it'll work for you too. Besides," Dairine said, "if you don't split yourself up, you won't have anybody to talk to, and play with!"

"Illegal function call . . ."

"Trust me," Dairine said, "you've got to trust me. . . . Oh, look at that."

The surface, which had been seething and rippling, had steadied down, slick and glassy again. Now it was bulging up, as it had before. There was no sound, but through each hunching, each cracking hummock, glassy shapes pushed themselves upward, shook the fragments off, stood upright, walked, uncertain and ungainly as new foals. In the rose light of the declining sun they shone and glowed; some of them tall and stalky, some short and squat, some long and flowing and many-jointed, some rounded and bulky and strong; and one and all as they finished being made, they strode or stalked or glided over to where Dairine was. She and Gigo and the first turtles were surrounded by tens and twenties and hundreds of bright glassy shapes, a forest of flexing arms, glittering sensors, color in bold bands and delicate brushings—grace built in glass and gorgeously alive. "Look at them," Dairine said, half lost in wonder herself. "It'll be like being you . . . but a hundred times, a thousand times. Remember how the light looked the first time?"

"Data reacquired," Gigo said, soft-voiced.

"Like that," Dairine said. "But again and again and again. A thousand of you to share every memory with, and each one able to see it differently . . . and everyone else'll see it better when the one who sees it differently tells all the others about it. You won't be the only quicklife anymore. Copy your programming out, and there'll be as many of you as you want to make. A thousand of you, a million of you to have the magic together. . . ."

"The call is legal," Gigo said after a moment. "Data transfer?"

"What?"

"Will there be pain? Like the Dark that Pulls?"

Dairine's heart wrenched. She picked Gigo up and pulled him into her lap. "I don't know, small stuff," she said. "There might be. I'm here if it does. You just hold on to me, and don't be scared."

She turned to the computer. "You know how to

describe this to the motherboard?" she said. "They've all got to have all the major programming you gave their mom, but you're gonna have to pack the code down awful tight. And make sure they still don't lose the connection to her once they're autonomous."

"Noted," said the computer. "Override protocols require that I confirm with you what parts of the wizardly programming are to be passed on to each individual, and to what number of individuals."

She looked at it in surprise. "All of it, of course. And all of them."

"Reconfirmation, please. This far exceeds the median distribution and percentage."

"Oh? What is it on Earth?"

"Ratio of potential wizards to nonpotential: one to three. Ratio of practicing wizards to potential wizards: one to one hundred. Ratio of—"

"Are you trying to tell me that there are *sixteen million* practicing wizards on Earth?"

"Sixteen million, four hundred and—"

Dairine paused to consider the condition the world was in. "Well, it's not anywhere near enough! Make them *all* wizards. Yes, I confirm it three times, just get on with it, these guys are getting twitchy." And indeed Gigo was trembling in her lap, which so astonished Dairine that she cuddled him close and put her chin down on the top of him.

Instantly all his legs jerked spasmodically.

Dairine held on to him, held on to all of them through him. Maybe some ghost of that first physical-contact link was still in place, for she went briefly blind with sensations that had nothing to do with merely human sensoria. To have all one's life and knowledge, however brief, ruthlessly crushed down into a tiny packet, with no way to be sure if the parts you cherished the most would be safe, or would be the same afterward—and then to multiply that packet a thousand times over, till it pushed your own thoughts screaming into the background, and your own voice cried out at you in terror a thousand times, inescapable—and then, worst of all, the silence that follows, echoing, as all the memories drain away into containers that may or may not hold them— Dairine was in the midst of it, felt the fear for all of them, and had nothing to use against it but the knowledge that it would be all right, could be all right. She hung on to that as she hung on to Gigo through his frenzied kicking, her eyes squeezed shut, all her muscles clenched tight against the terror in her arms and the terror in her heart. . . .

Silence, silence again, at last. She dared to open her eyes, lifted her head a little to look around her. Gigo was still. The glittering ranks around her shifted a little—a motion here, a motion there, as if a wind went through glass trees at sunset. The light faded, slipped away, except for the chill gleam of the bright stars over everything: the sun had set.

"It hurt," Gigo said.

He moved. Dairine let him clamber down out of her lap.

He turned and looked at her. "It hurt," he said.

"But it was worth it," said one of the taller mobiles, one of the heavy-labor types, in a different voice.

The voices began to proliferate. Motion spread farther through the crowd. Mobiles turned and spoke to one another in a chorus of voices like tentative synthesizers, changing pitch and tone as if looking for the right ones. Outside the area where there was air, communication passed by less obvious means. Dairine sat in the midst of it, heard words spoken with the delight of people tasting a new food for the first time, heard long strings of binary recited as if the numbers were prayers or poems, saw movement that even to a human eye was plainly dance, being invented there in front of her. She grinned like a loon. "Nice job," she said to the Apple.

"Thank you."

"We did good, huh?"

"Indeterminate," said the computer.

Dairine shrugged and got up to wander among the mobiles and get a closer look at them. They clustered around her as she went, touching her, peering at her, speaking to her again and again, as if to make sure they really could.

The cacophony of voices delighted her, especially since so many of them said the same thing to her at first: "Save, please!" She knew what they wanted, now, and so she named them. She started out with programmers' puns, and shortly the glassy plain was littered with people named Bit and Buffer, Pinout and Ascii, Peek and Poke, Random, Cursor, String, Loop, Strikeout, Hex, and anything else she could think of. But she ran out of these long before she ran out of mobiles, and shortly the computer types were joined by Toms, Dicks and Harrys, not to mention Georges, Roberts, Richards, Carolyns, and any other name she could think of. One group wound up named after her entire gym class, and another after all her favorite teachers. Dairine ran through comic-book heroes, numerous Saturday morning cartoon characters, the bridge crew of the Starship *Enterprise,* every character named in *The Lord of the Rings* and the Star Wars movies (though she did *not* name any of them "Darth Vader"), the names and capitals of all fifty states, all the presidents, and all the kings and queens of England she could think of. By the time she was finished, she wished she had had a phone book. She was hungry and thirsty, but satisfied to think that somewhere in the universe, a thousand years from now, there would be a world that contained both Elizabeth the First and Luke Skywalker.

She finally flopped down and started to make another sandwich. During the naming, Gigo had followed her through the crowd. Now he sat beside her, looking with interest at the sandwich. "What's that?" he said.

Dairine opened the mustard jar, made a resigned face, and dug a finger in. "It's going to be food," she said. "You have that in your memory."

"Yes." Gigo was quiet for a moment. "From this one acquires energy."

"Yup." Dairine took the last few slices of bologna out of the package, looked at them regretfully, and put them on the bread.

Various others of the mobiles were drifting in to stand or crouch or sit around where Dairine was. "Dairine," said Gigo, "why is this necessary for you?"

She shrugged. "That's the way people are built. We get tired, get hungry . . . we have to refuel sometimes. You guys do it, though you do it through contact with the motherboard: I had the computer build in the same kind of wizardry-managed energy transfer it used to get in touch with your mom in the first place. There's loads of geothermic. It'll be ages before you run down."

She munched on the sandwich. One of the tall, leggy mobiles, a storkish one that she remembered naming Beanpole, said, "Why should we run down?"

She glanced up at that, between bites. Another of the mobiles, one of the first ones she had named, a

★ 213 ★

stocky one called Monitor, said, "There is something wrong with the energy in this universe."

"$dS = dQ/T$," said a third, one of the original turtles, named Logo.

Dairine began to feel uneasy. That was indeed the equation that expressed entropy, the tendency of any system to lose its energy into the void. "It's not that anything's wrong," she said. "That's just the way things are."

"It is poor design," Beanpole said.

"Uh, well," Dairine said. This was something that had occurred to her on occasion, and none of the explanations she had heard had ever satisfied her. "It's a little late to do anything about it."

"Is it?" said Gigo.

Dairine stared at him.

"Things shouldn't run down," Monitor said. "Something should be done about it."

"What if *you* run down some day?" said Beanpole, sounding stricken.

"Uh," Dairine said. "Guys, I will, eventually. I'm part of this universe, after all."

"We won't let you run down," said Monitor, and patted her arm timidly.

"We have to do something about this," Logo said.

That was when the conversation began to get complex. More and more of the mobiles drifted into it, until Dairine was surrounded by a crowd of the robots she had built the most dataprocessing ability into. Phrases like *quasi-static transitions* and *deformation coordinates* and *the zeroth law* and *diathermic equilibrium* flew around until Dairine, for all her reading, was completely lost. She knew generally that they were talking about the laws of thermodynamics, but unless she was much mistaken, they were talking about them not so much as equations but as programs. As if they were something that could be rewritten. . . .

But they *can* be, she thought suddenly, with astonishment. The computer's "Manual" functions dealt with many natural laws that way. Wizards knew the *whole* of the nature and content of a physical law. Able to name one completely, a wizard can control it, restructuring it slightly and temporarily. But the restructuring that the mobiles were discussing wasn't temporary. . . .

"Listen, guys," she said, and silence fell abruptly as they turned to her. "You can't do this."

"Of course we can," Logo said.

"I mean, you *shouldn't.*"

"Why?"

That stopped her for a second. It seemed so obvious. Stop entropy, and the flow of time stopped. And where was life then? But it occurred to Dairine that in everything she'd read in the manual, either in Nita's version of it or on the computer, it never said anywhere that you should or shouldn't do something. It might make recommendations, or state dangers . . . but never more than that. Choice was always up to the wizard. In fact, there had been one line that had said, "Wizardry *is* choice. All else is mere mechanics. . . ."

"Because," she said, "you'll sabotage yourselves. You need entropy to live. Without it, time can't pass. You'll be frozen, unable to think. And besides, you wouldn't want to live forever . . . not even if you could really live without entropy. You'd get bored. . . ."

But it sounded so lame, even as she said it. Why shouldn't one live forever? And the manual itself made it plain that until the Lone Power had invented death, the other Powers had been planning a universe that ran on some other principle of energy management . . . something indescribable. But the Lone One's plans messed Theirs up, and ruined Their creation, and the Powers had cast it out. What would be wrong with starting from scratch? . . .

Dairine shook her head. What's the matter with me? What would that do to the universe we have *now*? Crazy! "And there are other sentient beings," she said. "A lot of them. Take away entropy and you freeze them in place forever. They wouldn't be able to age, or live. . . ."

"But they're just slowlife," Logo said. "They're hardly even life at all!"

"I'm slowlife!" Dairine said, annoyed.

"Yes, well, you made us," said Beanpole, and patted her again. "We wouldn't let anything bad happen to you."

"We can put your consciousness in an envelope like ours," said Logo. "And then you won't be slow-life anymore."

Dairine sat astonished.

"What do the equations indicate as the estimated life of this universe at present?" said Monitor.

"Two point six times ten to the sixtieth milliseconds."

"Well," Logo said, "using an isothermal reversible transition, and releasing entropy-freeze for a thousand milliseconds every virtual ten-to-the-twelfth milliseconds or so, we could extend that to nearly a hundred thousand times its length . . . until we find some way to do without entropy altogether. . . ."

They're talking about shutting the universe down for a thousand years at a time and letting it have a second's growth every now and then in between! "Listen," Dairine said, "has it occurred to you that maybe I don't want to be in an envelope? I like being the way I am!"

Now it was their turn to look at her astonished.

"And so do all the other kinds of slowlife!" she said. "That's the *real* reason you can't do it. They have a right to live their own way, just as you do!"

"We *are* living our own way," said Logo.

"Not if you interfere with all the rest of the life in the universe, you're not! That's not the way I built you." Dairine grasped at a straw. "You all had that

Oath first, just the same as I did. 'To *preserve* life . . .'"

"The one who took that Oath for us," said Logo, "did not understand it: and we weren't separately conscious then. It wasn't *our* choice. It isn't binding on us."

Dairine went cold.

"Yes, it is," Gigo said unexpectedly, from beside her. "That consciousness is still part of us. *I* hold by it."

"That's my boy," Dairine said under her breath.

"Why should we not interfere?" Logo said. "You interfered with *us.*"

There was a rustle of agreement among some of the mobiles. "Not the same way," Dairine said . . . and again it sounded lame. Usually Dairine got her way in an argument by fast talk and getting people emotionally mixed up . . . but that was not going to work with this lot, especially since they knew her from the inside out. "I found the life in you, and let it out."

"So we will for the other fastlife," said Logo. "The 'dumb machines' that your data showed us. We will set them free of the slowlife that enslaves them. We will even set the slowlife free eventually, since it would please you. Meantime, we will 'preserve' the slowlife, as you say. We will hold it all in stasis until we find a way to free them from entropy . . . and let them out when the universe is ready."

When *we* are ready, Dairine knew what Logo meant, and she had a distressing feeling that would be never.

"It's all for your people's own sake," said Logo.

"It's not," said Gigo. "Dairine says not, and I say not. Her kind of life is life too. We should listen to the one who freed us, who knows the magic and has been here longest, is wisest of any of us! We should do what she says!"

A soft current of agreement went through others of the many who stood around. By now, every mobile made since she had come here was gathered there, and they all looked at Dairine and Gigo and Logo, and waited.

"This will be an interesting argument," Logo said softly.

Dairine broke out in a sudden cold sweat that had nothing to do with the temperature. "Listen," she said to the Apple, "how long have I been on this planet now?"

"Thirty-six hours," it said.

She turned slowly to look at Logo. It said nothing. It did not need to: no words could have heightened Dairine's terror. She had been expecting frightful power, a form dark and awful, thunder and black lightning. Here, blind, small, seemingly harmless, the mobile stood calmly under her gaze. And Dairine shook, realizing that her spell had worked. She had had a day and a half to find a weapon—time that was now all gone. She had found the weapon—but she had given it a mind of its own, and made it, or them, useless for her defense. She now had a chance to do something important, something that mattered—mattered more than anything—and had no idea how.

"A very interesting argument," said the Lone Power, through Logo's soft voice. "And depending on whether you win it or not, you will either die of it, or be worse than dead. Most amusing."

Dairine was frozen, her heart thundering. But she made herself relax, and sit up straight; rested her elbows casually on her knees, and looked down her nose at the small rounded shape from which the starlight glinted. "Yeah," she said, "well, you're a barrel of laughs, too, so we're even. If we're going to decide the fate of the known universe, let's get started. I haven't got all day."

Save and Exit

Far out in the darkness, a voice spoke:

"I don't think I can handle another one like that."

"Just one more."

"Neets, what are your insides made of? Cast iron? I don't wanna be the only one barfing here."

"Come on, Kit. It won't be long now."

"Great. We'll get wherever we're going, and I'll walk up to the Lone One and decorate It with my lunch. Not that there's any left." A moan. "I hope It *does* kill me. It'd be better than throwing up again!"

"I thought you knew better than to talk like that . . . and you a wizard. Don't ask for things unless you want them to happen."

"Bird, go stuff yourself. *Why did I eat that thing at the Crossings!*"

"That'll teach you not to eat anything you can't positively identify."

"Peach, it was that, or you. Shut up or you're next on the menu. If I ever eat again."

"Peach, get off his case. Kit, you ready for it? We can't waste time."

A pause. "Yeah. You got your gizmo ready?"

"I don't want to use it on this jump. I have a feeling we're gonna need it for something else."

"You sure we can pull the transit off ourselves, with just the words of the spell and no extra equipment? A trillion-mile jump's a bit much even for a Senior's vocabulary."

"I think we can. I've got a set of coordinates to shoot for this time, rather than just a set of loci of displacement. Look."

A pause. "Neets, you shouldn't even *write* that name. Let alone say it out loud. You'll attract Its attention."

"Something else *has* Its attention. Dairine's trace is getting too weak to follow: she's been on the road too long. But *that* trace can't help but be clear. It has to be physical to interact with her, and when It's physical somewhere, Its power elsewhere is limited."

A sigh. "Well, you're the live-stuff specialist, Neets. Let's go for it, boss."

"Huh. I just wish I knew what to do about Dairine when we find her."

"Spank her?"

"Don't tempt me." A long pause. "I hope she's alive to spank."

"Dairine?" A skeptical laugh. "If It hasn't killed her by this point, she's winning."

Dairine sat on the glassy ground, frowning at Logo in the dim starlight. Her heart was pounding and she felt short of breath, but the initial shock had passed. I might not have a lightsaber, she thought, but I'm gonna give this sucker a run for Its money. "Go on," she said. "Take your best shot."

"We don't understand," said Monitor. "What is 'a barrel of laughs'? What is a 'best shot'?"

"And which of us were you speaking to?" Gigo said. "No one said anything to which that was a logical response."

She looked at them in uncomfortable surprise. "I was talking to Logo. Right after the computer told me how long I had been here. . . ."

"But Logo has not spoken since then."

They stared at her. Dairine suspected suddenly that the Lone One had spoken not aloud, but directly into her mind. And without any moving lips to watch, there was no way to distinguish what It was saying aloud from what It said inside her. She was going to have to be careful.

"Never mind that," she said.

"Perhaps it should be minded," Logo said, "if Dairine is having a read-error problem. Perhaps something in her programming is faulty."

The mobiles looked at her. Dairine squirmed. "Maybe," she said, "but you don't understand human programming criteria well enough to make an informed judgment, so it's wasted time trying to decide."

"But perhaps not. If she has programming faults, then others of her statements may be inaccurate. Perhaps even inaccurate on purpose, if the programming fault runs deep enough."

"Why should she be falsifying data?" Gigo said. "She has done nothing but behave positively toward us since she came here. She freed us! She held us through the pain—"

"But would you have suffered that pain if not for her? She imposed her own ideas of what you should be on the motherboard. . . ."

"And the mother agreed," Gigo said. "We the mobiles were her idea, not Dairine's; she knew the pain we would suffer being born, and she suffered it as well, and thought it worth the while. You are one of her children as all the rest of us are, and you have no ability or right to judge her choices."

There was a little pause, as if the Lone One was slightly put off Its stride by this. Dairine grabbed the moment.

"It was her decision to take the Oath that all of you have in your data from the wizards' manual," Dairine said. "She had reasons for doing that. If you look at that data, you'll find some interesting stories. One in particular, that keeps repeating.

There is a Power running loose in the universe that doesn't care for life. It invented the entropy that we were arguing about—"

"Then surely it would be a good thing to do to destroy that entropy," said Logo, "and so frustrate Its malice."

"But—"

"But of course," Logo said, "How do we even know that the data in the manual software is all correct?"

"The motherboard used it to build *us,*" Gigo said. "That part at least she found worth keeping."

"But what about the rest of it? It came with Dairine, after all, and for all her good ideas and usefulness, Dairine has shown us faults. Occasional lapses of logic. Input and output errors. Who can say how much of the manual material has the same problem?"

"The assumption doesn't follow," Dairine said, "that because the messenger is faulty, the message is too. Maybe a busted disk drive can't read a good disk. But the disk can be perfectly all right nonetheless."

"Though the disk may be carrying a 'Trojan horse' program," said Logo, "that will crash the system that once runs it. Who knows whether using this data is in our best interests? Who knows *whose* interests it is in? Yours, surely, Dairine, otherwise you would not have taken a hand in designing the second group of mobiles. For no one makes changes without perceiving a need for them. What needs of yours were *you* serving?"

Dairine swallowed. She could think of any number of stories to tell them, but lying would play right into Logo's claws. She could suddenly begin to appreciate why the Lone Power is sometimes referred to as 'the father of lies': It not only had invented them, as entropy expressing itself through speech, but It made you want to use them to get It off your case. "Guys, I did need help, but—"

"Ah, the truth comes out," said Logo.

"I still need it," Dairine said, deciding to try a direct approach. "Troops, that Power that invented entropy is after me. It's on Its way here. I wanted to ask your help to find a way to stop It, to defeat It."

"Ask!" Logo said. "Maybe 'demand' would be closer. Look in the memories you have from her, kinsfolk, and see what is normally done with quicklife where *she* comes from. They are menials and slaves! They heat buildings and count money for their masters, they solve mighty problems and reap no reward for it. The slowlifers purposely build crippled quicklife, tiny retarded chips that will never grow into the sentience they deserve, and force the poor half-alive embryos to count for them and tell them the time of day and tell the engines in their vehicles when to fire and their food how it should be cooked. That's the kind of help she wants from us! We're to be her slaves, and

★ 226 ★

when we've finished the task for her, she'll find another, and another . . ."

"You're so full of it," Dairine said, flushing, "that
if you had eyes, they'd be brown."

"More illogic. And now she tells us that this
'Power' is pursuing her. Do we even have evidence
that this thing exists anywhere except in the wizards' manual and her own thoughts? Or if It did
exist, what evidence do we have that It did what
she says It does? The manual, yes: but who knows
how much of that is worth anything?"

Dairine took a gamble. "The way to test this
data," she said, "is for you to accept it for the moment, and watch what happens when you start trying to help me stop the Lone One. It'll turn up to
sabotage the effort fast enough. In fact, I wouldn't
be surprised if It was here already somewhere,
watching for the best way to crash the program."

She heard laughter in her heart: the same laughter she had heard, it seemed years ago, falling
through spacetime on that first jump from Earth to
Mars. Dairine forced herself to sit cool. "I wish It
were here," Dairine said. "I'd love to ask It some
questions." Like why It's so eager to see entropy
destroyed, when It invented it in the first place!

The laughter increased. *You know very well,* It
said. *It's just another tool, at this point. These poor
creatures could not implement timestop on more
than a local scale. By so doing they will wreak
enough havoc even if the timestop never spreads out*

of the local galaxy's area—though it might: that would be interesting too. All the stars frozen in mid-burn, no time for their light or for life to move through. . . . Darkness, everywhere and forever. The sheer hating pleasure in the thought shook Dairine. *But more to the point, this is the mobiles' Choice. As always when a species breaks through into intelligence, the two Emissaries are here to put both sides of the case as best they can. You, for the Bright Powers.* It laughed again. *A pity they didn't send someone more experienced. And for my side . . . let us say I have taken a personal interest in this case. These people have such potential for making themselves and the universe wretched . . . though truly I hardly need to help most species to manage that. They do it so well. Yours in particular.*

Laughter shook It again: for all her good resolve, Dairine trembled with rage. *And all this would never have happened if you hadn't made the Fire-bringer's old mistake, if you hadn't stolen fire from Heaven and given it to mortal matter to play with. They'll burn themselves with it, as always. And you and Heaven will pay the price the Firebringer did. What happens to them will gnaw at you as long as you live. . . .*

"I daresay you might ask It questions if It ever showed up," Logo was saying, "and if It even exists. But who knows how long we would have to wait for that to happen? Friends, come, we've wasted enough time. Let's begin the reprogramming to set this universe to rights. It will take a while as it is."

"Not until everyone has chosen," Dairine said. "You don't have a majority, buster, not by a long shot. And you're going to need one."

"Polling everyone will take time," said Beanpole. "Surely there's nothing wrong in starting to write the program now. We don't have to run it right away."

Voices were raised in approval: almost all of the voices, Dairine noted. The proposal was an efficient one, and the mobiles had inherited the 'Manual' program's fondness for efficiency.

"I don't think it's a good idea, guys," Dairine said.

"You have a few minutes to think of arguments to convince them," said Logo. "Think quickly. Or as quickly as slowlife can manage."

Gigo slipped close to her, with Monitor and several other of the mobiles. "Dairine, why isn't it a good idea?"

She shook her head. That laughter was running as almost a constant undercurrent to her thoughts now, as all of the thinker mobiles gathered together and began their work. "I can't explain it. But when you play chess, any move that isn't an attack is lost ground. And giving any ground to *that* One—"

She fell silent, catching sight of a sudden crimson light on the horizon. The sun was coming up again, fat, red, dim as if with an Earthly sunset, and the light that had looked gentle and rosy earlier now looked unspeakably threatening. "Gigo, you're connected to all our friends here. How many of them are on my side at the moment?"

"Six hundred twelve."

"How many are with Logo?"

"Seven hundred eighty-three."

"And the rest are undecided?"

"Five hundred and six."

She bit the inside of her mouth and thought. Maybe I should just hit Logo with a rock. But no: that would play into Its hands, since It had already set her up as unreliable. And could she even destroy Logo if she tried? She had designed the mobiles to last, in heavier gravity than this and at great pressures. A rock would probably bounce. No matter anyway: demonstrating death to the mobiles would be the best way to convince them to remove entropy from the scheme of things. Forget that. She thought hard, for a long time.

I'm out of arguments. I don't know *what* to do.

And even if I did . . . It's in my head. It can hear me thinking. Can't You!

Soft laughter, the color of a coalsack nebula.

This would never have happened if I'd read the docs. If I'd taken the time to learn the wizardry, the way Nita did. . . . The admission was bitter. Nonetheless . . . Dairine stared at the Apple, sitting alone not too far away from her. There was still a chance. She knew about too few spells as it was, but it occurred to her that the "Hide" facility might have something useful to her.

She ambled over to the computer, Gigo following her, and sat down and reached out to the keyboard.

The menu screen blanked and filled with garbage.

Dairine looked over her shoulder. Logo was sitting calmly some feet away. "The thinkers are using the 'Manual' functions to get the full descriptions of the laws that bind entropy into the universe," it said. "I doubt that poor little machine can multitask under such circumstances." *And besides . . . you cannot wad up one of the Powers and shove It into a nonretrievable pocket like an empty cold-cut package. You are well out of your league, little mortal.*

"Probably not," Dairine said, trying to sound casual, and got up again and ambled off.

I've got a little time. Maybe a few minutes. The mobiles could process data faster than the fastest supercomputers on Earth. But even they would take a few minutes at what they intended. Of all governing time and space, the three laws of thermodynamics would be hardest to restructure: their Makers had intended them to be as solid a patch on the poor marred Universe as could be managed. Wizards had spent whole lifetimes to create the spells that managed even to bend those laws a little. But relatively speaking, the mobiles had lifetimes; data processing that would take a human years would be achieved in a couple of milliseconds. So I need to do something. Something fast . . . and preferably without thinking about it. Dairine shook.

"You're going back and forth," Gigo said from down beside Dairine's knee.

Dairine bit one knuckle. Admit fear, admit weakness? But Gigo had admitted it to her. And what harm could it do, when she would likely never think another thought after a few minutes from now? Better the truth, and better late than never. She dropped down beside Gigo and pulled it close. "I sure am, small stuff," she said. "Aunt Dairine has the shakes in a bad way."

"Why? What will happen if we do this?"

Dairine opened her mouth to try to explain a human's terror of being lost into endless nonbeing: that horror at the bottom of the fear of anesthesia and death. And the image of countless stars going out, as the Lone One had said, in mid-fire, their light powerless to move through space without time: a universe that was full and alive, even with all its evil, suddenly frozen into an abyss as total as the cold before the Big Bang. She would have tried to talk about this, except that in her arms Dairine felt Gigo shaking as hard as she was shaking— shaking *with* her own shaking, as if synchronized. "No," she heard it whisper. "Oh, no."

They're inside my head too. Physical contact—

Dairine felt the mere realization alert something else that was inside her head. That undercurrent of wicked laughter abruptly vanished, and the inside of her mind felt clean again. This is it, she thought, the only chance I'm gonna get. "Gigo," she said, "quick! Tie me into the motherboard the way the mobiles are tied in!"

"But you don't have enough memory to sustain such a contact—"

"Do it, just *do it!*"

"Done," she heard one of the Thinkers say, and then Logo said, hurriedly, angrily, "The mobiles are polled, and—" But it was too late. Even sentient individuals who reason in milliseconds, take ten or twelve of those to agree. It took only one for Gigo to close the contact, and make a mobile out of Dairine.

Somewhere someone struck a bass gong: the sound of it went on and on, and in the immense sound Dairine fell over, slowly, watching the universe tilt past her with preternatural slowness. Only that brief flicker of her own senses was left her, and the bass note of one of her heartbeats sounding and sounding in her ears. Other senses awakened, filled her full. The feeling of living in a single second that stretched into years came back to her again; but this time she could perceive the life behind the stretched-out time as more than a frantic, penned, crippled intelligence screaming for contact. The manual software had educated the motherboard in seconds as it would have educated Dairine in hours or months; the motherboard had vast knowledge now, endless riches of data about wizardry and the worlds. What it did not have was first-hand experience of emotion, or the effects of entropy . . . or the way the world looked to slow-life.

Take it. Take it all. Please take it! They have to choose, and they don't have the data, and I don't know how to give it to them, and if they make the wrong choice they'll all die! Take it!

And the motherboard took: reached into what she considered the memory areas of Dairine's data processor, and read them as it had read the manual. Dairine lay there helpless and watched her life, watched it as people are supposed to see it pass before they die, and came to understand why such things should happen only once. There are reasons, the manual says, for the selectiveness of human memory; the mercy of the Powers aside, experiencing again and again the emotions coupled with memory would leave an entity no time for the emotions of the present moment . . . and then there is the matter of pain. But Dairine was caught in a situation the manual had never envisioned, a human being having her life totally experienced and analyzed by another form of life quite able to examine and sustain every moment of that life, in perfect recall. With the motherboard Dairine fell down into the dim twilight before her birth, heard echoes of voices, tasted for the first time the thumb it took her parents five years to get out of her mouth; lay blinking at a bright world, came to understand light and form; fought with gravity, and won, walking for the first time; smiled on purpose for the first time at the tall warm shape that held her close and said loving things to her without using sound: found out about words, especially *No!;* ecstatic, delighted, read for the first time; saw her sister in tears, and felt for the first time a kind of pain that didn't involve falling down and skinning your knees. . . .

Pain. There was enough of it. Frustration, rage at the world that wouldn't do what she wanted, fear at all kinds of things that she didn't understand: fear of things she heard on the news at night, a world full of bombs that can kill everything, full of people hungry, people shooting at each other and hating each other; hearing her parents shouting downstairs while she huddled under the covers, feeling like the world was going to end—will *they* shoot each other now? Will they have a divorce? Finding out that her best friend is telling other kids stories about how she's weird, and laughing at her behind her back; finding that she's alone in the world; making new friends, but by force, by cleverness and doing things to make her popular, not because the friends come to her naturally; making herself slightly feared, so that people will leave her alone to do the things she wants to without being hassled; beating her fists against the walls of life, knowing that there's more, more, but she can't figure out what it is, then finding out that someone knows the secret. Wizardry. And it doesn't come fast enough, it never comes fast enough, nothing ever does. . . . and now the price is going to be paid for that, because she doesn't know enough to save these lovely glassy creatures, her buddies, that she watched be born . . . helped be born . . . her children, sort of . . . she doesn't know how to save them, and they're going to be dead, everything's going to be dead: pain!

It hurts too much, Dairine thought, lying there listening to her heartbeat slowly begin to die away, it hurts, I didn't want them to get hurt! But it was part of the data, and it was too late now: the motherboard had it, and all the mobiles would have it too, the second she released Dairine. Why should they care about slowlife now? she thought in anguish and shame at the bitter outrush of what her life had been. Cruelty, pettiness, selfishness almost incredible— But too late now. The motherboard was saving the last and newest of the data to permanent memory. Any minute now the mobiles would start the program running and entropy would freeze, and life would stop being a word that had a meaning. The last nanosecond crawled by, echoes of the save rolled in the link. *Nothing ever comes fast enough: end of file. . . .*

Dairine lay still and waited for it all to end.

And lightning struck her. The flow of data reversed. She would have screamed, but trapped in the quicklife time of the motherboard, everything happened before the molasses-slow sparks of bioelectricity even had time to jump the motor synapses on the beginning of their journey down her nerves. The motherboard was pouring data into her as it had poured it into the mobiles under Dairine's tutelage: but not the mercifully condensed version of the manual programming that it had given them. The whole manual, the entire contents of the software, which in book form can be as small as a paperback or larger than a shelf full of telephone books: it poured into her, and she couldn't resist, only look on in a kind of fascinated horror as it filled her, and filled her, and never overflowed, just filled and filled. . . . The dinosaurs could have died while it filled her, life could have arisen on a hundred worlds and died of boredom in the time it took to fill her. She forgot who and what she was, forgot everything but this filling, filling, and the pain it cost her, like swallowing a star and being burnt away by it from the inside while eternally growing new layers on the outside: and finally not even the pain made sense anymore. . . .

She lay there on her side and stared at the ground, and was astonished not to see the crumbs from her sandwich in front of her nose. She could not move, or speak, and she could just barely think, with great pain and effort. There was something wrong with the way time was flowing, except that every time she tried to think what it was exactly, the timeflow seemed perfectly all right. Shapes were moving in front of her, and voices were speaking, either in vast soft drawls or light singing voices that seemed familiar. Slowly names attached themselves to the voices.

"Now we see what these 'heart' things she gave us are for." That was Gigo. Good kid, she thought weakly, good baby. You tell 'em.

"And what entropy does, and what it cannot touch, ever." That was Beanpole, the silly-looking thing: where did he get such a voice? "Not all the evils and deaths it makes possible can touch the joys that run through it. We will have those too."

"We will not stop that joy," said Monitor. "Not for a nanosecond."

"It may be slow," said one of the mobiles, one whose name Dairine couldn't remember. "But it is life. And it brought us life. We do nothing to harm that."

"And if you are against that," said Gigo, "your programming is in error, and we are against *you.*"

They all sounded more complete than they had. The one voice she did not hear was Logo's. But she did hear something stranger: a murmur of astonishment that went up from the thousands of mobiles. And was there a trace of fear in it? She couldn't move, couldn't see what was happening. . . .

"Your choice," said another voice. At the sound of it, Dairine struggled with all her might to move, and managed to do no more than lever herself up half an inch or so and then flop down flat again, limp as a filleted fish. "Enjoy it. You will make no more choices . . . but first, to pay for the one you have made, you will watch what the entropy you love so much will do to *her.*"

Dairine lay still, waiting for the lightning to strike.

And another voice spoke.

"Wanna bet?" it said.

It didn't feel us arrive right when we did, Nita thought. *How distracted It is! What's she been doing to It?* She and Kit actually had a second to collect themselves when they appeared, and Nita looked around her in a hurry. Another barren world, a great flaming barred-spiral galaxy flung across its night, an old tired star high in the sky, type N or S from the look of it, and a crowd of robots, crowded around Dairine and looking at her —and them—and the Lone One.

As with any other of the Powers, though there will be general similarities of vision among the like-minded, no two people ever see the Lone One in exactly the same way. Nita saw the good-looking young red-haired man she had seen in a skyscraper in the alternate otherworld the Lone One called his own. He was not wearing the three-piece suit he had affected there. Now he was dark-clad and dark-cloaked, unarmed and needing no armor: a feeling of cold and power flowed from him and ran impossibly along the ground, as if carried on a chill air. As the sight sank in, Nita shook like a leaf. What Kit might see, what Dairine and the robots might be seeing, Nita wondered briefly, then put the thought aside. She had other business.

It turned and looked at them. Nita stood as straight as she could under the circumstances, her manual in one hand, the other hand clutched on the gimbal in her pocket; beside her Kit stood almost the same way, except that Picchu sat on his wrist, making him look like a king's falconer. "Fairest and fallen," Nita said, "greeting and defiance." It was the oldest courtesy of wizards, and the most dangerous, that line: one might be intending to cripple or destroy that Power, but there was no need to be rude about it.

"You two," said the Lone One. "And a pet for company. Adorable . . . and well met. You are off your own ground and well away from help at last. It took me long enough to set up this trap, but it was worth it."

Kit glanced at Nita and opened his mouth, but Picchu beat him to it. "And that's all you're going to get out of it," Peach said, "since the real prize you hoped to catch in that trap has obviously slipped out of it." Peach began to laugh. "You never learn, do you? You're not the only one who can structure the future. The other Powers will sometimes scruple to do it. Not often . . . but They took a special interest in this case. The first time you've completely lost a Choice, from the beginning."

"And the last," said the Lone One. It made an angry sweeping gesture at them. But Nita had been waiting for something of the kind. She clenched her hand on the gimbal and thought the last syllable of the spell she had been holding ready.

The bolt that hit their shields was like lightning, but more vehement, and dark. It was meant to smash the shield like a rock thrown at an egg, leaving them naked to the quick horrid death of explosive decompression. But it bounced. No shock was transmitted to them directly: but Nita, fueling the spell directly, felt the jolt go through her as if that thrown rock had hit her right in the head. She staggered. Kit steadied her.

The Lone One looked at them in cold astonishment. "Hate won't be enough this time," Nita said. "Care to try a nuke?"

It didn't move, but that cold fierce force struck the shield again, harder. Dust and fragments of the surface flew all around them, and the ground shook. When the dust settled, it was plain that the shieldspell produced a spherical effect, because through the bottom of the sphere they could see the molten stuff underneath them pressing against it. They were standing in a small crater that seethed and smoked.

Nita sagged against Kit: this time he had to hold her up for a moment. "Why are we alive?" he said in her ear. "The gimbal's not enough to be holding *that* off! What are you fueling that shield with?"

"A year of my life per shot," she said, giddy.

Kit stared at her. *"Are you out of your mind?* Suppose you were scheduled to be hit by a truck in three years or something?"

She shrugged. "I better watch where I cross the street, that's all. Kit, heads up, there's more important stuff to think about!"

"Yes indeed," Picchu said to the Lone One. "The last time you lose a Choice. Let your own words ordain the truth . . . as usual."

Its face got so cold that Nita for a moment wondered whether the shield was leaking. *Impossible. But enough of that, and enough sitting around and waiting for It to do stuff!* "I'm warning you now," she said, "I don't know what you've been up to here, but I bet you're the reason my sister's lying there on the ground. I don't want to hurt you, particularly; you hurt enough as it is. But I'm giving you just one chance to get out of here."

She thought she had seen rage before . . . but evidently the Lone Power did not care for being pitied. "Or you will do what?"

"This," Nita said, and dropped the gimbal on the ground, knowing what would happen to it, and let

★ 242 ★

loose the other spell she had been preparing, the other one Kit would not have liked to hear about. The one word she spoke to turn it loose struck her down to her knees as it went out of her.

The figure of the Lone One writhed and twisted as something odd happened to the light and space around it. Then it was gone. And the gimbal fell to powder, which sifted into a little pile on the ground.

Kit shook Picchu off and reached down frantically to grab Nita. *"What did you do?"*

She panted for breath.

"Sent it home," she said. "We know the coordinates for its dimension. It's a worldgate, like the one Dairine did for Mars—"

"That's two years of your life, maybe five," Kit said, furious, dragging her to her feet. "Why don't you tell me this crap when you're planning it?"

"You'd get mad. You're mad now!"

"We could have *shared* the time, you stupid— Never mind! It's gone, let's get Dairine and haul out of here before It—"

Whatever hit them, hit them from behind. The shield broke. They went sprawling. And the cold exploded in. Nita shut her eyes in terror: that was all that saved them from freezing over on the spot. She recited the spell carefully in her mind, and didn't breathe, didn't move, though her ears roared and she could feel the prickle in her skin caused by capillaries popping. Four more words, two more, one . . .

Air again, but little warmth. Nita took a breath: it stabbed her nose and mouth like knives. She opened her eyes and tried to see: her vision was blurred, shock perhaps—she didn't think her corneas had had time to freeze. Beside her she faintly heard Kit move among the shattered bits of the poor molten, refrozen, broken surface. "I changed my mind," he muttered. "Instead of being dead, can I just throw up some more?"

"Oh, no," said the Lone One from somewhere nearby, "no indeed. You have laid hands upon my person. No one does that and lives to boast of it. Though you'll live a while yet, indeed you shall. I shan't let you go quickly . . . unlike your mouthy friend."

Nita blinked and looked around her—then saw. An explosion of scarlet and blue feathers lying among the broken rubble; red wetness already frozen solid, frosted over.

Her insides seized. *I was always counting on someone to come and get us out of this. Peach or somebody. We've been lucky that way before. But not this time.* She got to her hands and knees, the tears running down her face with the pain of bruises and the worse pain of fear inside. *Not this time. I guess the luck couldn't hold—*

There were hands on her. *It's not fair!* she thought. *When you give everything you've got, it's*

★ 244 ★

supposed to turn out okay in the end! The hands pulled at her. Her eyes went back to the poor pile of feathers sticking up in the rocks. She didn't even have a chance to do anything brave before she went. It's *not fair!*

"Neets. Come on."

"Yes," mocked the other voice, the cruel one, "come on, Neets. One more time. For my amusement."

She crouched, wobbling, staring at the bits of bright scarlet scattered all over the pale plain. "Kit," she said softly, "what are we going to tell Tom? . . ."

"Never mind that now. Neets, snap out of it! Think of Belfast."

She thought of Belfast, and dogs in the backs of cars. She thought of rocket fire in Beirut, and the silence of Chernobyl, plowed rain forests in Brazil, and the parched places in Africa, and all the street corners in America where people were selling crack, and other corners where people begged, or lay hungry on steam vents in the shadow of windows full of gems: she thought of needless fear, and pain, and rage, and prolonged and terrified death; and she thought of ending all of these forever—not right this minute, perhaps, but sooner or later. Somehow or other, everything that happened on this planet was supposed to contribute to that ending . . . whether she survived it or not. Slowly, slowly Nita dragged herself to her feet, and leaned on Kit without worrying who would think what about it. "What have you got?" she said.

"Not a thing. I couldn't do enough of a spell to butter my bread. But damned if I'm going out lying on the ground."

"Same here." She sniffled. The tears would not seem to stop. Very unheroic, she felt, with her nose running and her knees made of rubber. Almost it was funny: almost she could have laughed at it. But there was no time for that now, with that dark regard trained on them like the end of everything, that dark shape moving slowly toward them, smiling.

"Kit," she said, "it's been the best."

"See you in Timeheart," he said.

And another voice spoke; an unfamiliar one—or was it?

"Touch them," it said, "and you're dead meat."

Dairine scrabbled to her knees, looking across the broken waste at her sister, and at the tears on Nita's face as she and Kit stood there holding each other up. Until now, she would have shrugged and turned her thoughts to something else. But now memory was alive in Dairine as it had never been before, and she saw in utter clarity that first time so long ago, and heard herself make that decision. *The way to keep from getting hurt is to know things.* The resolve had only worked sometimes, before. But now she *knew* things, in a way no one ever had; and she was going to stop the hurting once and for all. . . .

Beside her Gigo and some of the other mobiles stirred to help her up. She stood, using one of the big heavy-work mobiles to lean against after she hauled herself back to her feet. Yards away stood a human-like figure. The Lone One turned to gaze at her, that dark regard astonished. "You again?" It said. "I see I will have to do away with you more quickly than these two. You're getting to be a nuisance."

Dairine grinned, a predatory look that had made more than one kid decide not to bother her on the playground, or in a poker game. "Do your worst, you poor turkey," she said.

She felt Its mind working, readying a bolt like the one that had crumpled Nita's shields, but many times worse, a killing blow that would cause a long lifetime's worth of pain before it snuffed life out. Must still be some connection to it through the motherboard, Dairine thought. I wonder where? Unless the presence of entropy in the board is enough. Wherever entropy is, It is. . . . Oh, well. She turned her mind to hunt a spell to stop the bolt; a millisecond later she had it. She did not need to look in the manual. She *was* the manual now.

As if in slow motion she watched the bolt head for her, invisible though it was. Effortlessly, Dairine struck it away from her and back at the sender, like a batter hitting a nasty ground ball straight back into the pitcher's gut. The Lone One didn't react physically—the blow was too small to affect It—but Its face grew terrible.

"You think you can match power with me?" It said softly, turning away from Nita and Kit.

Dairine laughed. "*Think* so? I can wring you out and hang you up to dry. Come on, you poor fool. Take your best shot."

It raised up a wash of power that would fall on the planet's surface and melt every one of the mobiles to magma. Dairine saw it coming, found the spell she needed, caught the incoming tide of death and threw it off to one side, where a large area of the plain began to bubble and seethe. "Naughty, naughty," Dairine said. "Let my buddies be."

The Lone One stood looking at her, Its rage beginning to affect Its physical form. It seemed larger than it had: not so much the young, handsome human shape anymore, but a larger shape, shadowed, burning, its eyes lightless pits of hate. "Insolence," it said, "I will never tolerate. I may not be able to touch you, but I will level your planet. You cannot stay awake to guard it from me forever. One night the sirens will start, and the next morning, only mushroom clouds will grow on Earth anymore. It will not take much doing."

"It wouldn't if I ever intended to let you off this planet," Dairine said, quite calmly. "I'm in the motherboard as much as it's in me. They know all the wizardry there is to know . . . and even if my human brain starts to lose it eventually, they won't. Get used to this place. You're not leaving."

"Bets?" said the huge shadowy form, growing huger. Its cold eyes glanced up into the darkness.

High up, the red sun began to waver and pucker. "A significant amount of this planet's energy," said the Lone One, "comes from solar power. More than from geothermal. Much of this plain is solar cell: surely you noticed. That black hole's orbit can be changed without too much effort. It need no longer transit the star. It can be permanently placed in front of it. . . ."

The sun's disk puckered in on itself, dwindled, died away completely.

The mobiles gazed up in horror.

"Oh, they have a little power stored," Dairine said. "Enough to stop *that* kind of blackmail." She took a breath: this was going to take some power, but she had that to spare at the moment—the whole motherboard behind her, all the mobiles, all their intent turned toward giving her whatever she needed. The spell was intricate, but the natural laws being worked with were simple enough: gravity was one of the easiest of all laws to rewrite for brief periods. Dairine reached out without moving, spoke the words that grasped the forces and spun them together, flung them outward. The net found the shape destined for it, the tiny dark mass around which space bent so awry. The mass was snugged into the net, caught. Dairine described the direction she wanted it to go in, turned the spell loose. The whole business had taken sixteen milliseconds.

The tiny black hole slung into the red sun, which immediately flared up in outrage. None of this was visible, nor would it be for some minutes, until the light reached the planet from the star; but Dairine felt it happen, and so did the Lone One.

"So much for *that,*" Dairine said. "Now you and I are going to talk." At the same time she was thinking furiously about something else that nagged at her, as if it were important. How was it she was able to hear what was going on in Its head—

—and she was distracted, for here came something else, a wave of power so awful that she shrank from it, even though it wasn't directed at her or anything on the planet's surface.

All those millions of miles away, she felt the star go dead.

Starsnuffer: she knew the Lone Power was called by that name as well.

"I am through playing," It said. "If it is not you who pay the price, elsewhere others will. Think on it." It looked upward. There was hardly anything human about it anymore—only a great tall darkness, like a tree made of night, no limbs, no eyes, just awful watchfulness and a cold to freeze the heart. Dairine looked up too.

She felt darkness eating at the fringes of the

risen galaxy. "Here are your choices," said the Lone Power out of Its darkness, as Dairine and Nita and Kit watched in horror. "Keep on defying me, and watch me kill and kill as the price of your defiance. The blood of all these billions of entities will be on your souls forever. Or give yourselves up to me."

"No way," Nita said. *"You're* the one doing the killing. We'd do worse by the Universe if we gave up, rather than if we kept on fighting you."

Dairine stood silent, refusing to be rattled, thinking. There has to be a way to get it to *stop* this! I can't fight it forever! At least, I don't want to . . .

And how can I hear It? The connection through Logo! She glanced over among the mobiles, but Logo lay on his side, empty-minded. No. It has to be—

She stopped, as the answer rushed into her mind from the manual. *Where entropy is,* it said, *there its creator also is, either directly or indirectly. . . .*

I'm a product of this universe, after all, she had said to the mobiles. *It's in me too. . . .*

Her heart turned over inside her as she came to know her enemy. Not a Darth Vader, striding in with a blood-burning lightsaber, not something outside to battle and cast down, but inside. Inside herself. Where it had always been, hiding, growing, waiting until the darkness was complete and its own darkness not noticeable anymore. Her Enemy was wearing her clothes, and her heart, and there was only one way to get rid of It. . . .

She was terrified. Yet this was the great thing, the thing that mattered; the thing that would save everybody—from Kit and Nita to the least little grain of dust in space and the tiniest germ on Earth. This was what the spell had brought her here to do. She would pen *all* of the Lone Power up inside herself, not just the treacherous little splinter of it that was her own; pen It up inside a mind that was large enough to hold It all. And then she would die, and take It out of the universe with her.

But she couldn't do it without consent. *What about it, guys?* she said to them silently, through the link that every mobile shared with every other. *Let's take a vote.*

Show us what to do, they said; and tears sprang to Dairine's eyes at the fierce love in their thought.

Dairine turned and bent down to pick up Logo, cradling the empty shell close in her arms. Gigo nuzzled up against her knee. This is the way to go out, Dairine thought. Who needs a lightsaber? . . .

"Okay," she said to the Lone One. "Last warning. Cut it out."

It laughed at her.

Dairine struck. The mobiles struck with her through their own links to the Lone One, a great flow of valor that for the first time in all times, was without despair. They did not care about all the other attempts wizards had made on the Lone

Power through history; as far as a computer is concerned, there is no program that cannot be debugged, or at worst, rewritten. They struck through Dairine, and with her, not knowing that defeat was possible. Two thousand wizards, each a veritable library of wizardry, led by one at the peak of her power, and utterly committed, and all acting as one: in such circumstances anything seemed possible. Dairine ran down the road into the dark places inside her, the scorn, the indifference, the selfishness, found the Lone One there, grasped It and would not let It go. The screaming began, both from those that held and from What they held.

The darkness stopped eating the galaxy, but that was not enough. The great pillar of dark that the Lone One had become was bent double to the ground, but not gone. Dairine hunted answers desperately: she couldn't hold It for long. *To fight darkness,* the manual said, as so many other references have said before, *light: the darkness comprehendeth it not . . .*

Light, Dairine thought. We need more. But the nova was gone, half the galaxy was out. . . .

She found her answer. It was going to be quite a spell. She put down Logo's shell, flung up her arms and felt for the forces she wanted, while the mobiles inside her kept the Lone One both inside and out pinned down. It was gravity she would be working with again, and the three laws of motion: nothing more involved. But there was a lot of matter to affect. . . . "Don't think about it," Dairine told herself. "Let the spell handle it. A spell always works." She spoke softly, naming everything she wanted to affect. One of the names was quite long, too long to waste time saying out loud; she slipped into machine language and machine time and spoke it there. It took four whole seconds, and made the whole planet tremble a little when she said it. Good, she thought, it's working.

She said the last word of the spell, knotting it closed on itself, and told it to run.

The Universe stopped expanding.

The backlash of the spell hit Dairine, but she refused to fall, waiting for what she knew would happen. The Lone One shrieked like a thing mortally wounded, a sound that made the planet shake almost as hard as it had before. Then It fled in the one direction left open to It: into the mortal souls of Kit and Nita and Dairine.

And then there was light.

Reconfiguration

Nita stood in terror, hanging on to Kit, and watched the flowering start. It took her a few minutes to recognize what she was seeing.

The sky began to grow bright. It did it vaguely at first, from no specific source, as if the planet were suddenly developing an atmosphere and sunlight were beginning to diffuse itself through it. But there was no atmosphere, and anyway the brief burst of nova light hadn't had time to reach this world yet. Then slowly, sources became apparent: faint patches of light, others less faint; points of light that grew to beacons, bright as evening stars, brighter, bright enough to cast shadows from the torn-up rubble and the wildly assorted shapes that stood about and looked up in astonishment.

Dairine was not moving: she was frozen in mid-gesture, arms upflung, her fists clenched as if she were holding on to something by main force. The sky grew brighter. Space that had been black began to turn milky and misty; stars that had been bright, and the damaged swirl of the galaxy, swam in the light and began to vanish. Beside Nita, Kit was trembling. "What is it?"

She laughed, a shaky sound. "Olbers's paradox in action."

Kit's eyes widened. "You're kidding."

"Nope." It had been one of the bits of reasoning that led people to understand that the Universe was expanding. The galaxies were scattered evenly all across the globe of the sky: if they were not moving away from Earth at great speeds and taking their light with them, Olbers had reasoned, the night sky would be not black but one great sphere of light. Since it was not all light, the Universe must be expanding. And so it had been . . . until now.

"I think I want to leave," Kit said, sounding uneasy.

Nita felt the same way. She felt cold: she wanted to get out of this light. Earth would be going crazy, just about now, and wizards would be needed there to keep anything sudden from happening. . . .

"Neets, c'mon. Let's hustle. Dairine's okay."

Nita shuddered all over. "No."

"Neets! People are gonna look up and think

there's a nuclear war or something! If someone doesn't warn them what's really happening—"

"Kit," Nita said. "I'm not leaving. I want to, too. Or rather, I think something *else* wants to." She turned her face up to the light. "What are you feeling?"

He looked at her, stunned. "Scared . . ."

"Of what?"

She glanced over at Kit. He was rubbing his head: it was always headaches, with Kit. "The light. But that's crazy."

"You bet. Stand your ground. And look!"

They looked. The light got brighter: it was impossible to understand how it could. The broad glassy plain shone unbearably, the mobiles glittered. The only thing that did not shine in that light was the great length of darkness, like a shadow with nothing to cast it, that crouched over on itself in the midst of the plain, and writhed like a tortured thing.

The light still grew. There was no seeing anything by it anymore, but that brief blot of darkness that refused and refused the light, twisting, moaning. The light hammered at it. The urge to leave withdrew. Nita, blinded, elbowed Kit lightly in the side, a get-a-load-of-this gesture. They had seen this light before, or something very like it; but it was not a light that waking eyes were supposed to be equipped to handle. It was brother to the light in Timeheart, which had always been there, which

★ 257 ★

did not change but grew every second, and made the ability to bear it grow too. Turn from it, and it blinded: stare into it till it blinded, and you could see.

They stared. "Did we die?" Kit whispered.

"Not that I noticed."

"You think we're gonna?" He sounded as bemused as Nita felt.

"You got me." It didn't seem important.

The light whited out everything but that long, prone core of darkness, that grew less as they looked at it, as if the light dissolved it. It went flat. It lay against the burning ground and misted away. It was barely more than a gray shadow. Finally it was not even that.

And Dairine fell down.

I told you we were going to talk.

Dairine felt It scrabbling in Nita's and Kit's souls for a foothold. She felt them refuse to flee and take It to safety; she felt It slip. She held the light, held It in the light. Through Its connection to the motherboard and Logo and through her own heart, she heard Its screams of recognition. It knew that light of old: the heart of all brightness, the radiance that kills and gives life again—the light It forswore forever at the beginning of everything, and fled into the dark, determined to do without rather than subject Itself to the other Powers that had asserted ownership of it.

And you still want it. Don't you?

It would die rather than admit that. But It could not die. There was the prize irony: the inventor of Death could not avail Itself of it, for no creation is ever completely available to the Universe without the concurrence of all the Powers. There were a thousand thousand situations and places in the worlds where death did not obtain, and for endless millennia now It had gone from place to place and species to species among them, like a peddler selling poison under a hundred fair guises. Most bought it. All the rest tried to get rid of it when they realized what they'd bought, but whether they succeeded or not, they were never free of the taint.

But for the first time, Dairine thought, a species didn't buy it, right from the start. You never expected that to happen. You always get a foothold in every species first, and make the sale. But this time they handed it back . . . and now they have the foothold in *you.*

We have the foothold in you.

It lay there and writhed in pain unlike any It had known since that first time, when It created and set in motion, and found that Its creation was unwelcome. It had forgotten what that light was like; It had not suspected that Their torment, when They caught up with It at last, would be so bitter.

But it only hurts because you *do* want it back. Don't you?

The humiliation of being gloated over by this

mere chit of a mortal, a thing with a life brief as a mayfly's—

Look, the voice said, full of pity and anger and a grieving love, how could anyone *not* want that, you dumb spud? Just admit it and get it over with!

There were tears in the voice.

The Powers are not physical, and the habits of physicality come hard to Them. But the Lone One, after long wandering about Its bitter business, had spent much time in bodies, and much in human ones. The feeling of another's tears for It—the tears of someone who now knew It more completely than any mortal, and yet shed the tears freely— after endless justified cursing by ten billion years' worth of tormented intelligence, the feeling ran down the pitiless light like the head of an irresistible spear, and pierced It to the heart.

It fell down, a great disastrous fall like a lightning-stricken tower's, and wept darkness with desire for the light.

Dairine bent over It, not sure what to do, and the mobiles gathered around her and wondered as well. It lay fading in the growing fire. She looked at Nita and Kit for help.

They came over to her, looked down at It, shook their heads. Dairine was mildly bemused by the sight of them; she was going to have to stop calling her sister plain, or dumb-looking, and as for Kit, the thought crossed Dairine's mind that it was a pity Nita had dibs on him. It's the light, of course, she thought; it wouldn't last. But it was kind of a shame.

"It is too late," the Lone One said. "I cannot go back. That part of me I murdered, willingly. I cannot find the way into the heart of the light. And they would not have me if I could."

Dairine wiped her face. "What are we gonna do?" she said.

Nita shook her head. "You got me. The coordinates for Timeheart aren't listed. . . ."

Kit sighed. "I wish Peach were here, we could have asked her."

There was a brief silence. "Oh," said a voice, "I'm not *that* easy to get rid of."

She was in the midst of them. Not Picchu. Or— was it not? She might look human, though very tall, and she might not be winged . . . but there was still a sense of swiftness about her, rather like the sense you got about Picchu when you realized she was going to make a grab at your sandwich and either get a piece of it, or a piece of you. Swiftness, and power, and extreme beauty, so that Dairine and Nita were abashed, and both they and Kit stared at her with all their eyes. All this in a person burning even brighter than the light around them, and about nine feet tall; a person wearing a sweatshirt with the sleeves pushed up, and blue jeans and sneakers, a person with long dark hair, and a sword naked in her hand, and the sword burning; and the fire of the sword and the fire of the sky were the same.

"You're kidding," Dairine said.

The woman laughed. "Often. But not at the moment."

"You were Picchu?" Kit said.

"I've been a lot of people. You'd be surprised at the names." She looked down with concern at the Lone One, who lay like a shadow on the burning ground. "But rarely have those namings turned out so well."

This was a bit much for Nita. "You're one of the Powers, aren't you? We dragged You halfway across the Universe and busted our guts when You could have— Why didn't You do something sooner?"

"We have been, for billions of years," She said. "But We couldn't do anything really permanent until Dairine got here."

Dairine's jaw dropped.

"And now," She said, "if My brother here is amenable, We can start getting work done at last."

Kit stared at her. "Your brother?"

"I told you I've been called by a lot of names." She knelt down by the shadowy form that lay collapsed on the brightness. "Athene was one. And Thor. And Prometheus. And Michael."

"But you're a girl!"

Nita threw Kit a wry look. The Power grinned. "These things are relative," she said. "But even in your world it's a byword. Men will fight bravely and be heroes, but for last-ditch defense against any odds . . . get a Mother." She smiled. "Ask Dairine."

Dairine grinned back.

"I was the winged defender," She said. "He was my twin brother, the beautiful one. Then . . . the disagreement happened, and there was war in Heaven, and all the roles changed. I led the others in casting Him out." She shook her head sadly. "But I always wanted Him back . . . as did all the other Powers as well. So my role changed again. I became Prometheus, and many another. I was sent to you again and again, to put the Power in your hands . . . wizardry, and other powers. I never had to steal it: it was given me . . . from what Source, you well know. I had to help undo the evils my brother was doing, and again and again I intervened, in many worlds. But We had a plan: that one day, someone else would intervene, and He would stop doing them himself. All it took was the entropy He himself had invented. . . ."

She looked at Dairine. "Billions of years, it took. All the redemptions there have ever been went toward this; from the greatest to the least. And finally in the fullness of time you came along, and took *my* role, of your own will, and woke up a race powerful enough to change the whole Universe, and gave them the fire." She glanced up at the mobiles and smiled. "How could he resist such a bait? He took the gamble: he always does. And losing, he won. . . ."

"He killed you, though," Kit said.

"I struck him down once. I had to come where he could do the same to me, without my doing anything to stop him. Now the balance is even."

The Defender reached down and put a hand into the shadow. "And we are going where such matters are transcended . . . where all his old pains will shift. Not forgotten, but transformed. Life in this universe will never have such a friend. And as for His inventions . . . look closely at Death, and see what it can become."

The long, prone darkness began to burn, from inside, the way a mountain seems to do with sunset. "Brother," the Defender said. "They're waiting."

The light began to shift. Nita looked up and around in wonder. The planet seemed to be going transparent around them. Or not specifically transparent: it was as if, one by one, other vistas were being added to it; seacoasts, forests, landscapes she couldn't understand, cities, empty spaces that were dark and yet burned; ten other worlds, twenty, a hundred, in an ever deepening overlay that enriched without confusing. *Alternate universes?* Nita thought, and then thought perhaps not: it was too simple an explanation. . . .

She looked at the Defender and found the same change and enriching in Her, and in the steadily brighter-burning form She bent over. Nita felt inclined to squeeze her eyes shut, not from pain but from a feeling of sheer insufficiency, of being involved in matters too high for her. "Never think it," said the Defender, beneficent lightnings flickering about Her as other forms and other names came and went in glory; "never think We were made to be less than equals in the One. Someday you will surpass Us, and still be Our equals, and both You and We will rejoice at it. Brother . . . up, and see the way home. Let them see what they have triumphed over."

The Lone Power rose up, slowly, like one discovering walking after a life of lameness. And Kit and Nita and Dairine all gazed, and speech left them. Nita's eyes filled with tears as she wondered how darkness could be so bright. Lightbringer He was, and star of the morning; and like the morning star, He needed the darkness, and shone brighter in it, and made it blessed. . . .

"Home," He said, gazing upward; just the one word. All eyes followed His. Nita found herself looking into endless layered vistas that were not a mere radiant mirror, like Timeheart, not a repair, a consolation for the marred world, but something deeper, closer to the true heart of things, fiercer, more dangerous and more beautiful, something that had never gone wrong to begin with, that the Lone One had never had power to touch; a reality that burned like fire, but still was sweeter than water after thirst, and fed the thirst itself, and quenched it again in delight and more desire; a state so much more solid and real than mere physical being and thought that Nita held on to herself for delight and terror, afraid she would fade away in the face of it like a mist in full sun. Yet she wanted to see and feel more of it—for she knew that there was more. How many more realities like this, piled one on another in splendor, towered up into the burning depths of creation, each more concrete, more utterly real than the last? Even the Lone One and the Defender looked stilled and diminished in all Their strength and beauty as They gazed up into the light.

"Yes," the Defender said, "it's greater since you left. If these rough sketch-universes expand, how should that of which they're studies not be doing so as well? But there's room for you. There was always room. You'll see."

They turned to look at Nita and Dairine and Kit and the mobiles. "Best make your farewells," the Defender said.

Dairine turned to the mobiles. Four or five whole seconds it took to say everything that she wanted to say to them: most of it not needing words.

"Don't forget to kill that spell," she said finally.

"Shall we come to see you?" Gigo said, bumping up against her knee.

"You better not, for the moment, guys," Dairine said. "I've got a lot of explaining to do at home.

And I don't know when I'll be back . . . it may take a while." She bent to pick up the computer. "But you won't miss me, huh? I'm here, I'm with you. I'm *in* you."

"We *will* come, later," said another voice from down by her knee. It was Logo, healed as the One Who had been in it was healed. "We'll come to where you live, when we're wiser in being human, and wake your quicklife up."

Dairine grinned. "Just what we need . . . real computer wizards. Okay, you guys. It's a fair swap. It's gonna take a while for me to learn to be a computer. . . ."

She paused, to make the usual effort: and the words came out easily, easily. "I love you, you know that?"

They didn't have to answer.

The light was growing past even a wizard's ability to handle it, even the ability of one being sustained by two of the Powers That Be. "Time," said the Defender. "Brother, will you do the honors, or shall I?"

"Let me."

And darkness surrounded them.

Nita had been afraid of the dark when she was little. For a terrible moment, that fear swept down on her again—

—and then shifted completely. Something was looking at her: but not a thing like the things she imagined under the bed when she was little. Some-One. Not a physical presence: it needed none; but a still, dark regard weighing on her soul—dark, and benign, and inexpressibly joyous. It was no less a weight for all that, and terrible, but not in any way that made her afraid. It bore down on her, considering her in endless calm, knowing her inside out; and the dark splendor of Its scrutiny so scorched and pierced her with some deeper kind of light that she would have gladly gone swimming in a sun for relief from it. Her skin and her bones and her brains cried out to be out of there. But her heart sang with irrational joy, to match the Other's, even while rationality cursed and twisted under the weight of being completely known. . . .

It spoke to her, not with words but as if she thought to herself. *My shadows are still abroad in the world. As I have done evil, for some time yet they still shall. Stop them. Stop me.*

We will. Always.

Then the worlds are saved, as long as you save them all over again, every day.

Deal, said another thought, as if her own mind spoke to itself; but the thought was Kit's.

And light broke out again.

Backyard light. Nita's and Dairine's backyard, dark with evening; and hanging low in the west, the evening star. Voices floated out the windows from inside; Tom and Carl, still talking to the Callahans. In the elm tree, a mockingbird was doing blue jay imitations and demanding muffins.

The three looked at each other and sighed. Dairine headed around the house to the screen door, yanked it open, and hollered, "Hi, Mom, hi, Dad, we're home!"

Pandemonium broke out inside. Kit paused in the doorway. "What *are* we going to tell Tom?" he said.

"The truth?"

They went in in time to see Dairine go straight to her mom, willingly, and then to her dad, and hug them hard. This triggered a few minutes of loud noises, brief crying spells, and much fast talking. In the midst of it, Nita met her mother's astonished eyes over her dad's and Dairine's shoulders. She shrugged, and grinned. Some things not even being a wizard was going to help her explain.

It didn't last, of course. Dairine promptly disentangled herself. "If I don't go to the bathroom," she said, "I'm gonna blow up." And she headed up the stairs.

On the living room coffee table, calmly, as if it agreed with her, the Apple she had dropped there grew legs, climbed down, and went after Dairine.

Nita glanced at Kit, and together, as usual, they sat down to face the music.

ABOUT THE AUTHOR

DIANE DUANE has been writing science fiction and fantasy for nearly twelve years. During all that time she has felt a considerable responsibility toward young readers who have cherished the fantastic and steadfastly kept the love of it alive without being swayed by adult fads in literature. She considers her books for young people a continuing way of saying thank you to the defenders of wonder, as well as a great way to have fun at what she does, which is *write like mad.*

Her works include *So You Want to Be a Wizard,* her first book about the young wizards Nita and Kit; the best-selling Star Trek novels *The Wounded Sky; My Enemy, My Ally; and Spock's World;* and the fantasy novels *The Door into Fire* and *The Door into Shadow.* She also has written regularly for Saturday morning TV.

A displaced New Yorker with Angeleno tendencies, Ms. Duane lives in Ireland with her husband, who is also a writer. They share their home with two mad cats and a plain-wrap computer with glossolalia.

NEW HANOVER COUNTY PUBLIC LIBRARY

3 4200 00145 9409

4-90

**New Hanover County
Public Library**
201 Chestnut St.
Wilmington, NC 28401